Book 1: Faith

Tami Casias

OOMM Books

Sonoma, CA, 95476, USA

First Printing, October 2010

5 4 3 2 1

Copyright© Tami Casias, 2010

All rights reserved

ISBN: 978-0-9829735-1-6

Publisher's note:

This is a work of fiction. Names, characters, places, and incidents either are the product of the author's imagination or are used fictitiously, and any resemblance to actual persons, living or dead, business establishments, events or locales is entirely coincidental.

"A jewel of a debut." Deborah Halverson, author of

Honk if you Hate Me

Big Mouth

Writing Young Adult for Dummies (coming June 2011)

To my husband Glenn who has supported even my craziest ideas. To my daughter Caroline who sparked the idea for Julie's story on a long car ride to Ashland, Oregon. And to my other children Benjamin, Teresa and Joey who have listened patiently to numerous renditions. To my writers group Patricia Henley, Bonnie Lee, Julie Carlson and Carole Kelleher for the continuing therapy sessions.

I'd also like to thank Byron at Barking Dog Roasters who served up countless raspberry cookies and coffee refills –along with Matt, Liz and Emily at the Schellville Grill in Sonoma where they kept the nicoise salad, apple crisp and iced-tea coming during months of lunch hours while I wrote my story.

Format, layout and pulling his hair out by Glenn Casias
Cover design and photography by Benjamin Casias
Cover art by Teresa Casias
Jewelry Design by Caroline Casias
Special Projects by Joey Casias

www.tamicasias.com

Chapter 1

I cracked my eyes open to look out at the morning light. The window wasn't there.

Untangling my legs from the sweaty sheet, I sat up to find that I wasn't where I was supposed to be. My head at the foot of the bed and the pillow on the floor told me I'd had another one of those nights. The seven-year-old scenes reliving Mom's death didn't have to rush back into my head all at once. They lived there. Always.

Tangled brown hair, puffy eyes and a zit the size of a stop sign reflected in the bathroom mirror. I cranked the shower up to help beat out the bad dream and because I looked better in fog.

Dressed in new jeans, I squeezed around piles of unpacked boxes in the hall. We'd moved to Sonoma four days ago and only pulled out what we really needed. We were supposed to arrive before school started back in September. Dad promised me a full year in one spot, but he flaked and took a month-long job in Merced first.

So now it's Monday, October tenth and I'm about to have my second uncomfortable first day as the new girl this year. And, it's my birthday. Sixteen. No mother. No real home. And I could really use a first kiss.

Downstairs in the kitchen, Dad was fighting with a stack of coffee filters. The filters were winning. His curly blond hair stuck out around his shirt collar at odd angles. He needed another haircut.

"Why are you up so early?" I asked.

"I never went to bed."

"What happened to no more all-nighters?" I took the filters from his hand and got the coffee started.

"I was working on the mural plans for the city council chambers." He rubbed his eyes with his freckled hands and watched me shake two aspirin from the bottle. "What are those for?"

"I woke up with a headache." I quit trying to tell him about my nightmares a long time ago. Watching him cry did not make me feel better.

"Do you want to stay home? I'll be gone. You'd have the place to yourself."

Tempting...I'd put off the "new school crap." But I shook my head and swallowed the pills with a quick gulp of water. It would just be there tomorrow. "Have you heard from Gramma? She hasn't returned my messages."

"I bet she's busy with their new catalog. Give her a few days to call."

"Call? I'm expecting her to be here."

"Today?" His back was turned to watch the coffee drip directly into his cup. I couldn't see his face.

"You know," I flapped my hands in the air, "for my birthday?" Did he forget his only child turned sixteen today? Probably. It wasn't like he cared about anything but his work anyway.

"Oh...hmm." He kept his eyes on his coffee cup as he stirred in a spoonful of sugar. "Do you want to go out for Chinese tonight or maybe invite some friends over and I'll order pizza?"

Friends? Don't say what you're thinking Julie! I shivered as a whole bunch of goosebumps cropped up on my arms. "Chinese," I squeaked.

"Great. And did you get the laundry finished last night? I want to wear my blue shirt to the meeting."

He walked back up the stairs without waiting for an answer, balancing his overfilled coffee mug in one hand and a handful of freshly washed brushes in the other. I moved to the washing machine and talked to the wet clothes as I stuffed them into the dryer. "Invite friends? He dragged me here four days ago and he thinks I have friends? I haven't had a friend in seven years!"

I punched the start button, grabbed my backpack, and headed out the front door. The ancient blue wood on the porch steps squealed and I realized I was stamping my feet. Not exactly 'Sweet Sixteen.' I stopped, took a deep breath, and tried to think of something good.

The sun was warm on my face. That was good. I'd spent the last year in Seattle. Record rainfall. That was bad. Now I was wearing my first pair of low-rise jeans and a new pink shirt. All good. I made a birthday pledge to myself: "I refuse to think about my bad dreams, my lack of friends, or the next time I'll be crammed into a U-Haul."

There. I felt better. That is, until I noticed a woman pushing a stroller had stopped right in front of our house. She was staring at me like I was whacko. Okay, so that's not a big stretch. I attempted a smile and gave one of those little waves like I was riding on a parade float. *Mental note: No talking to myself in public!*

I hurried around her and made my way the four blocks to school. The tall, old two-story building sat in front of the main quad area. It was scattered with lunch tables and winged by rows of flat-roofed classrooms. Late Friday afternoon after school was out, I'd walked the quiet yellow halls and found all my classes. Today the school was so crowded I could hardly see the numbers on the doors.

At least I would know one person. My landlord was one of the sophomore English teachers—my first class of the day. Not exactly a ticket to popularity, but I'd take what I could get.

I rubbed my damp palms on my jeans before walking into the room. The pimple was on my left cheek, so I picked an empty desk on the left side a couple of rows from the front. I tried to blend into the wall while I checked out the class.

The room was stacked with books and looked the same as my last English class. The people were different yet somehow the same. It was too early to tell who the smart or nice ones were, but it was a cinch to pick out the female pack leader. She stood four inches taller than the other girls. Her tanned complexion was smooth and she waved a tiny pink pen in her manicured hand as she told a group of girls some story about gymnastics camp. One girl—a stick so thin that her head looked like it was too big for her body—called Miss Clear Face 'Kelly'.

Kelly had on the same pink shirt I did. Only, her boobs filled it out much better. Bummer. Perfect skin wasn't enough? Kelly turned to sit and a pink thong strap peeked out from her jeans. I grabbed at my hips and felt the top of my own plain white bikini bottoms. I pulled my shirt down and hoped no one had noticed.

Ms. Donovan was taking roll at the front of the classroom. She had long blond hair that hung in wild curls around her face. I would've killed for curly hair–probably because the hair genes in my family grew more like uncooked spaghetti. Some guys in the class gave each other a head nod when she turned to pick up a pencil off her desk. I guess a good body canceled out old age for them. The woman was almost as old as my dad, thirty at least. But she was nice.

"Goodwin, Jewel Anne," she called out.

"Just Julie please," I rasped.

"That's right," Ms. Donovan looked up and smiled at me. "Are you and your dad all settled in now?"

"Yeah, I guess." *Did we have to talk about this now?*

"Great."

The door opened as the tardy bell rang and I watched a kid with shaggy blond hair walk in. He stuck a thick drawing pencil like the kind my dad uses behind one ear. His grass-stained pants slipped lower on his hips with each step. I hoped he'd get to a seat before they were around his knees.

"You're late again, Eddie," Ms. Donovan said. "Take your seat." She pointed to the desk in front of me.

He looked right at me and smiled. "Hey, new girl."

I avoided eye contact and met Kelly's gaze, which then dropped to my pink shirt. Her look said we weren't going to be friends.

Ms. Donovan continued with the roster and then started to talk about some book I hadn't read yet.

At the end of the period, I took my time stuffing my backpack with three new books and waited to be the last one out. But Kelly stood in the doorway.

"Hey, uh—Julie is it?" she said from the front of the small group of girls. "I'm Kelly and these are some of my friends. We've staked out a table for lunch. Come sit with us and we'll fill you in on what's up at this school."

She was actually friendly. I must have read her wrong. But before I could think of some cool response Kelly said, "I can help you with your color choices. Just between us, you might want to stay away from pink. It really isn't your color."

I swallowed hard and tried to find my voice. Finally, I croaked, "Thanks. But I always do my homework at lunch."

"Whatever." Kelly's chin seemed to drop a little, then she looked right past me and a huge smile appeared on her face. "Hi, Jason!" she yelled and walked around me, trailing little Kelly wanna-be's.

I couldn't help it. I turned to look. *Wow!* The cutest smile I've ever seen was attached to a fabulous face and surrounded by wavy brown hair. I watched him pull a tube of lip balm out of his pocket and slowly roll it over his mouth—careful to cover every spot. I wanted his kiss. Not that it mattered. The hug Kelly gave him said she was his girlfriend. *One of probably fifty reasons why he'll never even talk to me.*

By the time I got to Spanish class, the only seat left was in the front row. The friendly Senor Otero smiled kindly at everyone but spoke so fast, I couldn't keep up with what he was saying—in English. The headache came back during the last ten minutes of class. I gave up listening and counted down the minutes on the wall clock. Finally Senor Otero said "Adios." That I got.

In the library, I pulled out a book at random, then sat in a corner with my back to the room and set up the props—the book Fun in New Zealand, my notebook and a pencil. I learned one thing from Seattle, Merced, and all the other towns Dad dragged me to: It wasn't as important to belong as it was to *look* like I belonged.

Last year I picked up a book on crocheting and actually read it. In my spare time—which was all the time—I taught myself how to crochet and ended the year with twenty-two scarves. I don't really wear scarves much, but I looked busy.

I leaned my elbows on the table and rubbed the headache at my temples. What a relief it would be to stay in one town long enough to make a real friend. Someone who would hear my life story and not think I'm a freak.

Icy goose bumps raced up my arms like park ducks after bread crumbs. *What is with my skin today?* I was digging through my backpack for a sweater when a girl with light brown hair and huge blue eyes plopped down at the table. She wore the widest straw hat I'd ever seen.

"Okay if I sit here?" she asked, then wrinkled her nose and leaned forward. "The guys on the other side have awful B.O. My name's Cathy—just plain old Cathy. I tried to change it to Caitlyn last year, but everyone still called me Cathy. You're Julie, right? You're in my Spanish class."

"Oh." *I really need to work on my conversation skills.* I pulled on the sweater and rubbed at the goosebumps on my arms. "I don't remember."

"That's because I sit in the back so I can see everyone. You can't be cold. It's roasting in here." Cathy took off the hat and played with the black ribbon. "Don't you just love this? I bought it at a vintage store for only a dollar."

"Uh...it's great. I think I'll move out of the air conditioning." I gave a smile that said 'don't waste your time talking to me' before moving across the room. By the time I sat down at another table my teeth were actually chattering.

"Is this warmer for you?" Cathy asked as she sat down and smiled, her lips forming a perfect heart.

I think I nodded. *If I just don't say anything she'll go away.* Opening my book to the first page, I tried to turn the second page but my hands were shaking too fast to grasp the paper.

"Wow, you're shivering," Cathy babbled. "I remember being that cold before. My brothers were trying to turn me into a living snowman."

My ears started to ring as I looked from my dancing goose bumps to my shaking hands to Cathy's mouth moving. "I have to go!" The few steps to the girls' bathroom felt like I was walking the wrong way on an escalator.

For several minutes I sat shaking from cold and missing Mom all over again. "Crap." I left my backpack at the table.

"Are you okay?" came Cathy's voice. "Wow, this is the nicest school bathroom I've ever been in—and it's so clean. It's my first time in the Library. The bathrooms at my last school were so gross; I'd never drink anything so that I could hold it all day."

She followed me into the bathroom? "What?"

"You've been in here a long time. I got worried," Cathy said. "I've got your backpack and your book. So why are you reading about New Zealand? Are you going there?"

I wiped the tears off my cheeks. I couldn't think of an answer for the stranger on the other side of the stall door who happened to have my backpack.

"Are you sick?" Cathy asked. "Should I get someone for you?"

"No--no," *The last thing I need is more people in here.* "I'm coming out."

I avoided eye contact while I washed my hands in the incredibly warm water. When I reached for my backpack I managed to drop it on the floor, my pencils and pens spilling across the floor. I bent to pick them up. "You'd think on my birthday something would go right."

"Your birthday? Wow. That's great. Are you fifteen too? I'm fifteen and a quarter, but I'm still waiting for my boobs," she pulled her shirt tight and looked at her figure from the side. "I'm still just an A. That's okay though because I want to be a full B by my sixteenth birthday."

"No, I'm sixteen." *I might as well say it now and get it over it.* "I had to repeat fourth grade." That was the year Dad kept forgetting to take me to school.

"Sixteen, cool! Are you getting your license? Do you have a car to drive? We could go everywhere!"

This girl was bizarre. "I haven't taken any of the driver's training classes yet." What I didn't say was that when your mom is killed by a hit and run driver, your Dad isn't anxious to get you behind the wheel.

"So today's your birthday." Cathy paused putting on lip gloss and caught my reflection in the mirror. "That's really great. I love my birthday. I like to stretch it out a whole week. What are you going to do? Having a party?"

"If you call going out for Chinese food with my dad a party."

"Just two of you? What's up with that?"

I tried not to sound as pathetic as I was. "Well, my Gramma's supposed to come too. I just moved here. I haven't met anyone yet."

"I moved here last month! I'm the youngest of six kids." Cathy rolled her eyes. "And the last one at home. My folks made me retire with them. On my birthday my mom always makes my favorite food for breakfast. What does your mom do?"

I hate this part. "My mom died when I was nine."

"Oh, I'm sorry." Cathy's smile dropped and she squeezed my arm.

"Thanks." Was there a rule on how long you had to keep up a conversation with someone who saved your backpack?

The bell rang and I headed for the door.

"You still cold?" she asked.

"No, no I'm not. I feel okay now." I was surprised it was true. I did feel okay.

By the time we stopped at Cathy's algebra class, she had insisted we trade phone numbers. It took me a minute to remember where I'd written it in my notebook.

"Hey," she said, "I'm going with some friends to Mary's Pizza Shack after school. Want to come?"

She already has friends? "No, I can't. I have to get home and wait for my gramma."

"Okay, we go a lot. You can come next time." Cathy pulled open the door to her next class. "And Happy Birthday!"

I ran off to P.E. glad I wasn't required to dress on the first day. Just outside the double doors leading into the gym, I stopped and stared at the large recycling bin. The torn sheet of binder paper with Cathy's number on it was still clutched in my right hand. I dropped it in. No point making friends I'd just have to leave.

Heavy textbooks dug the straps into my shoulders after school. When I finally reached home, the front door swung wide open and my Gramma Aurora wrapped her bracelet-covered arms around me, backpack and all. "Gramma!" I missed these hugs and sunk into the scent that always hung around her—like French vanilla and peppermint.

"Oh, my birthday girl." Gramma stood back to take a good look at me. We were almost the same height. "I'm so excited. Now I can finally tell you."

"Tell me what?" I pushed myself free.

"I've sure missed you," Gramma laughed and pulled me into the kitchen. "First tell me how you felt today. Anything unusual?"

"What are you talking about?"

"Maybe a bad case of hiccups, uncontrollable sneezes, flatulence, hot flashes, severe goosebumps…?"

I flinched.

"Ahh, goosebumps. Just like your dear mother, rest her soul. I had hot flashes. That was okay when I was young, but they threw me for a loop when I began menopause." Gramma leaned close and whispered, "Thought I had my powers back."

"Powers? What are you talking about? Did you start on the Corona early today?"

"Shh," Gramma hushed. "Your dad will be down any minute and he mustn't hear."

"Hear what? That my Gramma thinks she has powers? What powers do you have?"

"Oh, I know I don't have special powers anymore." Gramma looked quite serious. "Now you have them."

"Me?" The Oreo's on the counter called to me so I grabbed a handful. "And what am I going to do? Fly like Superman? Spit spider webs from my wrist? Cast magic spells?"

"Don't be ridiculous, Jewel Anne, and stop watching so much television." Gramma shook her head. "It's better than that!"

I twisted one cookie open and popped the dry half into my mouth.

"You're growing into your legacy," she whispered and looked around like someone might be spying on us. "You're a Changer."

Chocolate crumbs sputtered out over my shirt as I choked on her words. "A what?"

"Here comes your dad. We'll talk more tonight." She bent and started digging in the cabinet under the sink.

"But Gramma—"

"Tonight."

Chapter 2

Although my stomach was full, a familiar emptiness re-appeared when Dad pulled our old red car into the driveway after dinner.

"This is a nice town, but I have to believe that all of this moving around is hard on Julie," Gramma said to Dad.

"Julie never complains. Right?"

"That's true." *I keep everything inside where it slowly tortures me.*

"Sorry I didn't have time to find a gift," Dad added. He'd given me $50 in a plain white envelope. "But this way you can choose for yourself. What more could a girl want?"

I shivered as I climbed out of the car and rubbed at my arms. He had no idea how long my list was—friends, family, a love life.

"You can't be cold," Gramma wrapped an arm around my shoulders. "It's a beautiful evening. Just look at that full moon."

Just above the top of the mountain, the bright yellow moon sat like a tennis ball on an ant hill.

A phone rang from inside. "That must be for me," Dad took the steps two at a time, unlocked the front door, and disappeared inside. When I passed him on the way to the kitchen, he handed me the cordless phone. "It's for you."

Who's calling me? I stared at the phone in my hand, then looked at Gramma and then Dad and shrugged. "Uh, hello?"

"Hi Julie, it's Cathy. I left my Spanish book in class and my mom always makes me do my homework the day it's assigned. I told her we only have that class every other day, but she won't let me put it off. It's so junior high. Could I borrow your book tonight? I could bring it back tomorrow."

"Uh, yeah. You can borrow it. I finished already. There wasn't much."

"Awesome. My mom says she can bring me over in a few minutes. I'm sure we're not far away—this town is so little—but she won't let me walk anywhere alone at night. Is it okay?"

"Uh, sure. We just got back from dinner."

"Great. I'll be right over. Tell me where you live."

I gave her my address and returned the phone to the cradle. Then I followed the voices into the kitchen.

The smell of chocolate filled the room as Gramma lifted a large cake from a bright pink box. I knew it would be a rich mousse. She had brought it from New Orleans from the same bakery where Mom had always gone.

Several small bittersweet chocolate curls sprinkled onto the countertop. I picked one up and let it melt on my tongue as I imagined Mom standing next to me, sticking candles deep into the frosting. *God I miss her.*

"I don't know why you do this every year," Dad said to Gramma. "There are plenty of good bakeries outside of New Orleans."

"This cake is exceptional and so is Jewel Anne's birthday. They just go together." Gramma reached into her purse, pulled out a gift, and handed it to me. "Drew, would you run to my room and grab the bag of party plates I left in the closet?"

The packaging was from the catalog jewelry company Gramma owned with her best friend Rose. After Rose's husband died last year, she had moved into Gramma's extra bedroom.

Tugging on the purple ribbon, I lifted the lid off the small jewelry box. Inside lay a small clear crystal centered between delicate silver wings and suspended on a fine chain. "It's beautiful." I twirled it up to the light and watched the colors dance. "I don't remember seeing this in your catalog."

"That's because I designed it years ago for your mother. The crystal came from my mother's friend. She was a Changer too. I gave it to your mom on her sixteenth birthday. I know she would want you to have it today."

"Thank you so much." I decided to ignore the part about Changers. The necklace felt cool on my skin and I shivered as Gramma fastened the latch.

Dad returned with the plates. "Who was on the phone?" He froze in his steps and stared at the necklace at my throat.

Oh, God, he's gonna cry. Again. Distract! "It was a girl I met at school today. She's coming over to borrow something." I ran upstairs and grabbed the book. I took my time coming back down hoping Dad had pulled himself together.

The bell rang as I passed the front door. When I opened it, all I could see were balloons.

"Happy Birthday, Julie!" Cathy peeked her head through the large bouquet.

"Whoa." I reached for the ribbons that held the mass of Mylar. "You didn't have to do this."

"Yeah, right. It's your birthday. You need presents. This is my mom Dolores." Dolores had blue eyes just like Cathy and the same smile. But she was about four inches taller and quite a bit rounder. Cathy walked past me into the box-filled living room. "You haven't unpacked yet? I could help."

"Spanish, Cathy. We're here for the book, remember?" Dolores shook Gramma's hand and then mine. "Where did you find such a beautiful necklace?"

My hand rose to my throat and I touched the now warm crystal. "It was my mom's. Gramma just gave it to me for my birthday."

"It's really unique," she said to Gramma.

"Thank you," Gramma said. "I'm Aurora and this is my son-in-law, Drew. Would you like to come in? We have an enormous cake and the coffee's almost ready."

"No thank you, this is your family time. We wouldn't want to intrude."

"Nonsense. You've turned it into a party, as it should be."

At one end of the table, Dolores, Gramma, and Dad talked about retirement, art, and the jewelry trade. Thank God Cathy sat at the other end with me. She talked about what she was going to wear to school tomorrow, annoying monthly pimples and the best places in town to buy donuts. I nodded my head a lot.

After a serious dent had been made in the cake, Dolores pulled Cathy from her chair. "She needs to get home and finish her homework. Thank you for a delicious evening."

"Want to come over after school tomorrow?" Cathy asked. "I live a few blocks from here. We could stop by the bakery, or—"

"Thanks, but Gramma's here. I think I should—"

"Jewel Anne," Gramma said. "Of course you may go to your friend's tomorrow. I don't mind. Besides, it will give me some quality time with my son-in-law."

"Okay." *What else can I say?* "I guess if you don't care."

"Happy Birthday again," Cathy said. And then she did something weird. She hugged me. So did Dolores.

"Welcome to Sonoma," Dolores said. "Now don't be strangers. Come on by anytime."

I stood in the doorway and waved goodbye. When I turned around, Dad was already gone. *To his precious work, no doubt.*

"What a warm family," Gramma said. "I don't know when I've felt so welcome. Good choice, Jewel Anne."

"I didn't choose Cathy," I shrugged. "She sort of chose me."

"Think what you like. But I noticed your goosebumps just before the phone rang. Could it be you were wishing you had someone besides your old Gramma and dad to spend your birthday with?"

"Gramma, you're freaking me out again." *She really is.* I carried the balloons up to my room and tried to stay away from her for a while.

I'd missed my grandmother during the past six months. But as I stood outside the guestroom thirty minutes later, I wasn't sure I really wanted to go in. Changers and powers—that was just too weird. Old people sometimes had mental problems. I didn't want to think Gramma had fallen completely off the wall.

The door flew open. "Don't stand there," Gramma said. "Come on in." It was hard to believe, but in just a few hours the room had been completely transformed. No suitcases were in sight. The open closet door showed her clothes hanging in a neat row. Framed pictures covered the dresser top and a bright red quilt blanketed the bed.

"How do you do this?" I asked.

"What?"

"Make it look like you've lived here for years when you just got here."

"I always bring a little bit of home with me wherever I go. Come sit here. We have a lot to talk about." Gramma patted the quilt beside her and then unfolded a family tree from her worn Bible. "Did your mother ever mention her powers?"

"Never." *And I wish you'd quit doing it!*

"Then this is going to seem a little strange to you. But don't worry, everything will be all right. Now let's see. Where should I start? Right…here." Gramma traced a branch of the family tree to a leaf with my name on it. "As you can see, you're not the first only child in this family. Your mother was, and I am." I watched Gramma's slender brown-spotted hand as it moved from branch to branch across the lists of names. "What you probably don't know is how common it really is. As you can see here, and here," she pointed to the top, "it always happens in groups of three—three generations. It happens in other families too— like my friend Rose—all with ties to Three Rivers Plantation outside of New Orleans. Anyway, within these groups lies the power of change. For three years between sixteen and nineteen, each is given a gift—the ability to transform her life and the lives around her for the better.

"The young girl—no longer a child, but not yet a woman—has the ability to view the world with two sets of eyes. She can clearly see things that need to be changed around her and within herself."

This is scary. Gramma's losing it. I squirmed toward the edge of the bed, my eye on the door.

"We're each given a sign that helps us identify need," Gramma reached out and pulled me back before continuing. "Then it's up to us to determine what should occur. Generally, the input starts out to help you better enjoy your own life, and then it expands to others. This is where it can get overwhelming. You'll need to learn how to control it or you'll go crazy—too much input, you know.

"I've heard the most powerful of the women can also affect changes in the future and even the past. But, for myself, I had my hands full with the present. Although your mother was a very private person, I sensed she was much stronger than I was. I do know she helped an elderly neighbor reconnect with her family. She was very proud of that."

"Did you forget to take your meds?"

"I know this is a lot to soak up at once. But it will be so wonderful for you. Since you left New Orleans, you've kept to yourself. On my visits, I've never seen a friend and you haven't unpacked many of your boxes. Then suddenly, on your sixteenth birthday, the thing missing most from your life—friendship— shows up with a bunch of balloons. This isn't magic, but it's powerful." Gramma set the book on the bed beside her and folded her hands on her lap. "What else? Oh yes. Changes can only be made to improve life. They have to be within your lifetime and you can't change anything that has already been changed." She stopped and stared at me. "Here I've been talking and talking and I bet you have a thousand questions."

I chewed on my bottom lip and pressed my back against the headboard as I tried to respond. "You're telling me, that I'm part of a long line of witches…"

"Not witches, dear, Changers."

"I'm supposed to believe I am a Changer, with some special powers?" I started toward the door. "I don't want to hurt your feelings, but I really don't believe you. I'm the least powerful person I know. I'm going to bed now."

"I expected denial. Your mother reacted the same way." She followed me up the stairs. I couldn't shake her. "I won't waste time trying to convince you. The next few days will do that for me. I only wish I could stay longer this time."

I walked through the bedroom to the bathroom and closed the door.

Leaning against the door I let out a long breath as her footsteps trailed away. "Wow, she's nuts!" I said to my reflection. Although I had grown taller over the summer, my straight hair and ordinary brown eyes said nothing special. I sighed and took a closer look at the pimple of the day. "If I had the power to change things, would I look like this?"

Chapter 3

The silent morning kitchen suited my mood—cranky. I wasn't ready for company. Gramma's strange words had replayed over and over in my head last night, keeping me awake for hours.

At a sound from the stairs, I hurried out the door. I didn't want to talk to anyone this morning. Today, I would slip into the background and everything would return to normal. Maybe I'd see that cute Jason again.

Just as I reached the corner, the light turned red and a small black dog barked at me from behind a short white fence. I jumped. It's not that I don't like dogs. They don't like me. The ones that don't bark, sniff at my butt. *What that's about?*

A cool shiver ran up my arms and I heard a voice from behind. "Hey, new girl," he said. I turned to face Eddie, the tardy guy from English.

He dropped a half-smoked cigarette at my feet and twisted his torn black Vans back and forth over the stub. "How's it going?"

I gave a half smile and shrugged. My lousy morning had just managed to get even worse. *The last person I need to talk to today is a stoner.*

Eddie's chin dropped. "Don't worry. I'm leaving." He turned and crossed quickly against the light.

What's up with him? I crossed the street. *It must be the smoking.* Eddie spun around to face me, blocking the sidewalk. I stared at a crack in the cement near my shoe to avoid eye contact.

"Where do you get off judging me?" Eddie snapped. "Here I thought I'd be the nice guy and talk to the new girl and all you do is judge me."

"I didn't say anything." I stepped around him. "I just want to get to class." A*nd get away from you.*

"Get away? So that's how its gonna be, huh?"

I walked faster. He sped up too. When I slowed down, I couldn't shake him. I focused straight ahead.

The tardy bell rang as I reached geometry. The entire class—including Jason and his still luscious lips—turned and watched us at the door.

Eddie grinned and tucked his hands in his pockets. "See ya later, babe." He strutted to his desk.

My face felt so hot it must have been bright red.

"Who's that?" Jason asked Kelly as I passed.

The cutest guy in school notices me now?

"Nobody," Kelly said. "Just Eddie's new girlfriend."

Great!

Math wasn't my best subject—more like the worst. At least the list of problems helped take my mind off weird Eddie. But as soon as I walked into the quad for break, he stood right behind me. "Hey new girl."

Please stop! "Why are you following me?"

"Well, you seemed so interested in my life this morning," he said. "I figure you must be interested in me."

"But I didn't say anything."

"Whatever." Eddie smiled, enjoying my stress. Dirty hair fell over his blue eyes. "We obviously need to spend more time together, so you can get to know the real me."

Cathy stepped between us and faced Eddie.

"Hi, I'm Cathy," She grabbed his hand and shook it. "We haven't met, but I just moved here, too, and Julie's my new best friend. I'm sure you won't mind if I borrow her for awhile now, would you?" She pulled me away from him, all the way across the quad, near the vending machines. "You looked like you needed to be rescued."

"Thanks. I don't know what's with him. I saw him this morning on the way to school. He kept talking to me, but I ignored him. Now he says I said something that makes him think I want to know all about him."

"Ignore him," Cathy grabbed the arm of a tall skinny guy with dark hair that was walking by. "This is my friend Thomas. He's lived here forever. He's an A student if you need any help on homework, and his mom owns Plaza Bakery—they make the best sourdough bread. He's the first one I met in Sonoma."

"Are you going out with Eddie?" Thomas asked.

"No," I coughed. "I don't even know him. Why?"

"I heard Kelly tell someone a minute ago by the Coke machine," Thomas said.

"And you believe *that* gossip?" Cathy shook her head and looked toward Kelly's table. There was a crowd of girls around her, looking at her like she was the queen of their court. "She thinks she's 'all that' since she's the only one on the cheer squad who went to an expensive gymnastics camp this summer."

"Great." *Now I'm gossip.* I saw Eddie again, walking with an older guy that even from a distance had the greasiest hair I've ever seen. "What's Eddie's story?"

"I don't know," Thomas said. "He used to be pretty cool until about a year ago. He dropped out of baseball and started hanging with Randy—a dealer."

The bell rang and everyone scattered to class. Cathy and I walked to Keyboarding and sat next to each other. Kelly was already in the classroom and came over.

"I thought I would give you some advice," Kelly said with a large smile. "There's a lot you don't know yet about who's going out with who. You wouldn't want to get yourself into trouble. So if you have any questions, just ask me."

"Uh, okay," I shrugged. *What is she talking about?*

"You're obviously going out with Eddie now, so I shouldn't have to worry about you, right?"

"We're not going out," I said. *Like if I had a choice I'd choose Eddie over someone like Jason. What does he see in you anyway?*

Kelly's smile turned into a glare. "I just wanted to warn you."

She walked back to her seat and wrote something down on a piece of paper and passed it to a big guy next to her. He smiled and passed it on. Each reader turned to look at me after reading the note. When the page reached Cathy, she read it, tore it and put the pieces into her pocket.

I slumped behind the old fat monitor on my desk. I tried to concentrate on finger placement until my head ached. After ninety painful minutes, the bell rang. I hurried out, ignoring Cathy's call, and headed straight for the library.

In the back corner, I collapsed into a chair, put my face in my hands, and tried to figure out what had happened to my carefully built bubble today. I jumped at a touch on my shoulder.

"I thought I'd find you here." Cathy sat down. "I can't believe Kelly talking about your 'problems'."

"What problems?" Not that I didn't believe I had issues. I just didn't know which ones she was talking about. "What was in the note?"

"She's such a liar," Cathy said. "Everyone knows Eddie spent last summer with his grandmother while his mother was out of town. His mom's been living like a hermit since his dad ran out on them. Nobody ever sees her. Kelly wrote that you and Eddie hooked up over the summer and now there may be a little Eddie coming along soon. Don't worry, I told them I knew for a fact you just met him, that you think he's a loser, and that considering you're on your period now, I'm certain you're not pregnant."

I groaned. "You told everyone…"

"I wasn't going to let her talk crap about you. I know you wouldn't do anything like that. I can tell. I have a way of knowing these things. It's a gift. Let's go call her on it right now." Cathy stood and grabbed one strap of her backpack.

"No, please! I don't want to make a big deal out of it." I snatched the other strap and pulled. "Let's just ignore her."

"Okay," Cathy sat back down. "But I know what I would do!"

So much for staying in the background.

Chapter 4

Gramma's eyes widened to a ridiculous size as my story unfolded after school. I wished she would blink.

"I had no idea," she said finally.

"That teenagers could be so mean?"

"No." Gramma beamed. "That you would be so powerful."

"Awww Gramma! I've already had a really crappy day and I don't want to hear any more voodoo stuff."

"Just like your mother." Gramma laughed and I swear, I could've thrown my books across the room. I couldn't remember ever having been mad at her before.

"I'm glad to see my problems are so entertaining to you. Maybe I can fall and break my leg and then you'll really have something to laugh about."

"I'm sorry dear." Gramma closed her mouth tightly, but I saw the corners tug into a smile. "I didn't mean to laugh, I'm just excited. I've heard legends, but I never really believed. I'm so happy."

I squeezed my eyes shut. Gramma was losing her mind and I feared it was genetic.

Dad came into the kitchen. "What's going on?"

I looked at Gramma's dumb smile and then to my hands, I didn't realize I was holding the counter edge so tight, my knuckles were white.

"I'm just telling Julie how special I think she is."

"Oh. Well." He seemed to fumble a moment, then peeked under the table. "Julie, have you seen my black shoes? I can't find them. Also, I hoped you could iron my shirt. I want to look presentable tomorrow and you do a much better job than I do. Hey, what did you have in mind for dinner?"

I rubbed at the sudden chill from my arms. "Pizza for dinner, shoes are in the laundry room, and leave your shirt here, I'll iron it later. I'm going to do my homework." Grabbing my backpack I headed upstairs. *I wish I could be in a regular family where I am the teenager, not the mother.*

"Julie!" Dad said.

"What?" I turned around to look at him. His eyes were watering. My shoulders sagged. *What now?*

"What do you mean, 'what'?"

"I didn't say anything!"

"I watched your lips mouth the words!"

"I –uh-" *I know I didn't say it. I know I was thinking it.* Before I could deny it again he continued.

"I've been trying to be father and mother. I've done the best I can. I'm just not cut out for this, but I thought you understood and wanted to help. I never wanted you to resent me."

I couldn't connect any of the words swirling around my brain to whatever makes them come out of my mouth. I looked from Dad's twisted face to Gramma's huge smile. *I didn't say that out loud, did I?*

"I don't know what you're talking about," I said slowly, the way you speak to someone who has no clue. "I don't resent you. I'm going upstairs now. I'll call for pizza in about an hour."

Everyone was being so weird today—like they could read my thoughts. In the safety of my room, I perched on a box next to one of two windows and tried to settle down. I pulled open the white shade and stared out at the early rising moon.

Five minutes later, Gramma came in and sat on the edge of my bed, facing me. "How long have you been doing all the housework?"

"I don't know," I shrugged. "About a year I guess. Since I could walk to the store by myself. He was pretty lame at it anyway. When he isn't hungry, he figures I'm not either."

Gramma walked to the window and stared out. "He's been so fragile since my Marina left us. You'd never guess how alive he used to be."

"I don't get it. What set him off tonight?"

"He's never heard your feelings before."

"What feelings?" An odd-shaped cloud floated in front of the window and I tried to decide if it looked like a hippo or a marshmallow Peep. "I just said pizza for dinner. That's not very deep."

"It's not what you said. It's what you thought."

"What does he think I was thinking?"

"I don't know. I couldn't hear it, but he could."

I twisted on the box. Gramma had that goofy smile going again. "What do you mean?"

"What were you thinking?" she pushed.

I stared at my hands. It was easier to think bad thoughts about your dad, than having to say them out loud to your grandmother. "I've had the worst day. I guess I thought how nice it would be if I could be the teenager and not the mother."

"Ouch. That must have been tough for your father to hear."

"But that's the point, Gramma. I didn't say it. I thought it. He couldn't have heard me. You didn't hear me and you were right there. He must have read my body language or something."

"It's not complicated." Gramma sat on the bed. "The power is strong with you. Your heart has identified things that need changing in order to help others. Your thoughts about what's wrong are being transferred to the person who needs to hear them the most."

"You're telling me people can read my mind?"

"Some people can hear your thoughts, yes."

I dropped my face into my hands and shook my head.

"Think about it, Julie. Doesn't that explain some of the strange things that happened to you today? Some people heard your thoughts about them. Accept it. You have a special gift. You'll be able to help others. Maybe you'll even be a leader."

Warm tears rolled down my cheeks. "I don't want to be a leader. I just want life to go back to regular crappy." My nose started to run and I got up for tissue. I locked myself inside the bathroom, and Gramma out. Maybe she wasn't the one losing it. Maybe the crazy one was me.

Chapter 5

I tried to concentrate on homework, but after an hour the smell of pizza filled the room. I didn't want to face my over-sensitive father or whacked-out grandmother again, but my growling stomach drew me into the kitchen. It took a second to believe what I was seeing.

The small table was set with three places—real plates, not the paper ones we normally used—and a large salad bowl. I didn't know we even had one of those. Gramma was taking a pizza piled high with vegetables from the oven.

"Where did you get that?" I wanted to talk about pizza and nothing else. "I've never seen a pizza that big before."

"I made it myself."

"You're kidding. You didn't have to go to all that trouble for us. I would have ordered one. Dad never comes down anyway."

"Maybe I can change that." Gramma placed the hot pizza on the table and cut it into wedges. "Remind me to tell your dad the garbage disposal isn't working."

"I heard you." Dad walked in. "What's that heavenly smell?"

"Homemade pizza," Gramma announced. "Wash your hands and sit down."

Like he'll do that.

He spun and fixed his eyes on me. "I don't know what's gotten into you Jewel Anne, but I'm already tired of it." He sat down and talked to Gramma. "You went to all this trouble; of course I'll join you."

I sunk into a chair and tried to focus only on my grandmother's movements as she cut the still steaming pizza, scooping loose vegetables back onto each slice. *There is no way he could hear what I'm thinking, right?* I piled some salad onto my plate and then closed my eyes and concentrated on wanting someone to pass the dressing.

"Why are your eyes closed?" Dad asked.

"Uh," I stammered. "I just wanted the dressing."

"You just have to ask," Dad passed the ranch dressing. "It's not as if I can read your mind."

Whew! Okay. Gramma's just freaking me out again. I took a mouthful of pizza so large, I wouldn't be expected to talk. But they did, for hours it seemed, until Dad went back upstairs and Gramma disappeared into her room behind the kitchen.

I knew Gramma wanted to talk to me. But I didn't want to, yet. So I did something easier—the dishes. Unfortunately it didn't take long enough and soon I had no choice but to drag myself to the guest room where I stood in the doorway.

"Before you say anything, Gramma, I don't believe you. I thought real hard about wanting one of you to pass the dressing and no one did."

"Come here dear, sit with me." Gramma held a photo album on her lap and she patted the quilt next to her. I stayed in the doorway. "The power brings change to those who need it the most. It does not bring you salad dressing."

The only changing I looked forward to was changing the subject. The photo album didn't look familiar to me, but stepping in the doorway a bit, I could see pictures of Mom. I went in all the way and sat down. Gramma smelled like warm pizza.

"I don't remember these pictures." I touched one of Mom. "She looks so young and serious."

"Yes, only a few months older than you are now. I was on a buying trip to San Francisco and she wanted to come along. Here's a good one." Gramma pulled out a picture where Mom stood smiling in front of an old stone building. "We drove up to Sonoma Valley for the day. She was reading a Jack London book and wanted to see where he had lived."

"Mom was *here*?"

"It was the first time she was excited about anything since her powers started, so I was happy to bring her. She was very serious that first year."

I groaned. *Stop already.*

"I know it's hard to understand, but you must believe and learn to accept that Changing is now a part of you. Only through acceptance will you learn to control the powers and harness them to help others. My strength was weak. So were the signals telling me who I could help. The people who seemed to hear your thoughts today are the first people who need your help." Gramma squeezed my hand. "Think about your relationship with your dad."

"Do I have to?" She made a clucking noise as I stared at the floor. "What do you want from me? I'm just a kid."

"Jewel, most people have to change what they can and accept what they cannot. You don't have those boundaries. Think about the people who could hear your thoughts today and think about what seems to be wrong with their lives."

Give me a break! "Fine. What do I do? Wiggle my nose or blink my eyes?"

"Don't be sarcastic. And stop watching so much TV. It's not your eyes or nose that has the power! It's your heart. Which is why I was never able to change that grade in chemistry. No matter how hard I wanted it to change from a D to an A, in my heart I knew the only way I deserved an A would be to study." She shook her head.

Gramma's face looked sincere and her voice sounded soothing, but believe? No way. The phone rang and I jumped to answer it. I hoped it was a long phone survey of what teenagers really think about their families. I had a lot to get off my chest.

"What's up?" Cathy asked. "I didn't see you after school. I was going to come by your house, but then I saw the cutest boys at the Plaza. They were visiting from Australia or something. I traded email addresses with this blond guy named Nick. He was sooo hot! So where were you?"

"I saw Eddie and I thought he was waiting for me, so I walked home the long way. I'm sorry I missed you."

"Well, tomorrow night we're going to the movies and you're coming. Thank God it's Friday. I wish we didn't have class tomorrow. I don't think I can handle another day of school this week."

"Tell me about it." We went over the entire day and how I had been dumped on—how unfair it was and how I didn't deserve it. We talked for maybe an hour, long enough for Gramma to shut off her light behind her door, and Dad to be totally holed up in his studio.

Later, when I snuggled into my covers, it felt good knowing I had Cathy on my side. She knew a bad day at high school was worse than a bad day anywhere else. I thought about school and Cathy as I drifted off to sleep.

I sprang out of bed, slapping both hands over my mouth. I looked at the clock. Only minutes had passed since I'd drifted off. The nightmare had started out the same as always. The screeching brakes, the impact, and my mother's words: "I need to tell you…tell you…" But this time she'd actually finished the sentence: "tell you about Change."

Chapter 6

Gramma's parting words 'remember to accept.' My plan: forget she even came to visit.

It's usually sad when Gramma leaves, but as I walked to school I felt relief. I hoped by Christmas she would be normal. A cold breeze blew my hair and a whiff of pot into my face. *Pew. Gotta be Eddie.*

"You smell me before you see me?" Eddie walked up to the corner beside me. "What's up with that?"

"I didn't mean…I mean…" *I have to stop talking to myself.* "Well, you do smell like pot. If you're taking hits before school, you should expect people to notice."

"So you think I'm stoned? Do I look stoned?"

I looked into his brown eyes—clear and normal. From what I knew from TV, potheads had very red eyes.

"Shows all you know." He walked past me to cross the street. "Not everybody's life is as perfect as yours."

Perfect? My life is so miserable. I wish I could disappear. Eddie stopped so fast I ran into him. I froze in the middle of the crosswalk. He stared at me like he could see into my heart, then turned and walked off.

I stood in the same spot until he was far enough away and jumped when a car honked at me. The light had changed to red and I hurried out of the street.

Between English and keyboarding I thought of a plan. If I did have powers around Kelly, Eddie, and Dad—*if!*—then what I needed to do was avoid Kelly, Eddie, and Dad. Simple as that. When I was stuck with them in class, I'd just think about something else—like the Pledge of Allegiance.

Later I walked confidently into science class and took my seat. *I can handle this.*

"Quiet down class," Miss Day said, as she wrote questions on the wipe board. "Take out a sheet of paper and a pencil. We're having a pop quiz on measuring instruments."

Moans filled the room as backpacks zipped open and shut and the quiz got underway. I looked past Kelly to Jason. He chewed on his bottom lip as he wrote his answers. *The most kissable guy ever!*

Kelly's head swung around so fast, I heard her neck crack. "Are you trying to get into a fight?"

"What?" I asked.

She leaned closer and hissed, "Forget about his lips. Understand?"

Gramma was right—I'm a freak!

I stared down at the blank page. After several minutes, students began taking their completed exams up to the basket on

Miss Day's desk. I scribbled down some answers and then asked for a bathroom pass. Miss Day pointed to a large wooden marker shaped like a beaker hanging by the door.

Locking myself in a stall, I put the seat down and stared at the hook on the door. I rubbed at a headache clamped down on both sides of my head. My eyes squeezed shut and I searched for direction.

Just believe? Is that what Gramma said? Accept that they need my help and I'll know what to do? Ignoring everything hadn't made it any better. What now? Accept? I rubbed my temples some more. *Fine.* I'd give the acceptance thing a try and if it didn't work, I'd quit school and work at a circus.

Back in class, I took my seat again. Miss Day had just assigned a section to read, then bent over a stack of papers on her desk and played with a silver chain around her neck.

From behind my book, I glanced sideways at Kelly. This time the goosebumps skipped up my arms. I rubbed at the annoying spots and prayed they'd disappear. Then they spread over my whole body. *Okay, okay! I accept.* I stared at Kelly, resisting the urge to wiggle my nose and blink. *Kelly, what in the world do you want?*

I hate my life!

I jumped and knocked my book to the floor with a loud thud as I heard Kelly's words. She'd said them, but her mouth hadn't moved. She looked at me, frowned, and then turned back—one hand on her book and the other running through her long hair.

I can hear you, do you know that? I tried. No response. *Hello, Hello.* She did not seem to hear, but her thoughts were loud and clear. At least to me.

I haven't waited since sixth grade for Jason to realize I'm not his sister only to have some cute new girl get him.

I'm cute? Wait! *Focus, Julie.* Embarrassed that Kelly heard what I thought about Jason's lips and scared that she would kick my butt, I hid behind my book, chewed on my thumbnail, and listened.

Her mom and dad were in Europe. Again. And when they were home, they shipped her off to different camps. The only thing perfect in her life, she thought, was her skin.

After class, I waited for Cathy at one of the quad tables and used my notebook as a fan.

The cold morning had turned into a warm afternoon. My brain was hot and tired. *If the things I'd thought weren't real are, then what is?* A group of girls behind me were talking to Cathy. I couldn't join in. Between the shock of realizing I'm circus material and the flour tortilla of my cold bean burrito stuck to the roof of my dry mouth, I couldn't speak even if I could think of something to say.

Their talk turned to the Homecoming dance—what to wear and whose parent would be the least embarrassing to drop them off. It wasn't something I needed to worry about.

Eddie sat on the ground with his back against the wall. He had his knees propped up to hold a small sketchbook. His hand worked fast across the page. I slapped at the chills that began to crawl up my arms. If I didn't ask him he'd hear me thinking about him again. *What's up Eddie? What do you need from me?*

She was so sick this morning I thought she was going to die. I looked around. He was so loud someone must have heard. But no one did.

"Hey, loser!" Kevin said to Eddie as he walked by.

Eddie reacted with a lazy extension of his middle finger. It was black where he held his pencil. *Go screw yourselves,* he thought. *If you had to deal with half of what I have to, you'd bust into little pieces. If it wasn't for art, I wouldn't come to school at all.*

Chapter 7

I hadn't planned on running home after school. I wasn't even in a particular hurry. But the closer I got to home the faster I walked until I stopped, winded on the front steps, to unlock the door. I wanted to shut out all the strange things that had happened to me.

Dropping my backpack in the entry, I leaned against the front door to catch my breath and decide where to collapse. I craved security and comfort.

The couch was an explosion of books so I went into the kitchen but the table was covered in a collection of drying paint brushes. I searched for a snack to take up to my room. A note on the cookie bag read: "Gone for a couple of hours. Here's money to buy groceries. Dad."

A wet drop hit the note. A tear. Mine. I have no one to turn to, no one to hold me. "I can't even drown my panic with cookies," I sobbed. "We're out of milk."

"Ring." Just seeing Cathy's name on the caller ID made me feel better.

"Hey, you busy?" she asked.

"No."

"Come on over. Meet me at the corner."

Within five minutes we had steered around the Plaza Park ducks that followed our tracks with beady eyes and we were cutting across the deep green grass under the shade of the trees, crunching crisp leaves underfoot to the front door just as Cathy's dad—a tall lean man with completely white hair—walked out of the garage with a rake in his hand.

"Hi, girls." He stretched out his free hand. "You must be Julie. I'm Jacob. Cathy's told me about you. What's on the schedule for today?"

"Not much," Cathy replied. "We're going to hang out in my room and listen to music."

"Music? Is that what you call that hip-rap you listen to?" Jacob turned to rake the leaves into a pile. "I thought you were learning chants for jump rope. My sister used to always sing—*Not last night but the night before*," he bobbed his head forward chanting, "*twenty-four robbers came a knocking at my door.*"

"Cut it out Dad. You'll scare the neighbors," Cathy moaned. "Ignore him Julie."

The second I stepped into the front room, I was home. There were no piles of boxes, just comfy-looking furniture and family photos everywhere. It smelled good, too. I didn't know what was cooking but I hoped I'd be invited to stay.

"Hello," Dolores said. "Dinner will be ready at five. Can you stay Julie?"

"Uh…" Had Dolores heard my thoughts too? "I guess."

"Come on Julie," Cathy said. "Let's grab some cookies and go to my room." A sound of rumbling came from the hallway and before I knew what was happening, a large brown animal had his large paws on my waist and was licking my face. "Ugh!" I tried to push it off without really touching it. It didn't work. "Get it off!"

Cathy tugged on the collar and pulled the animal down to all fours. From a distance of several feet, I could see it was a dog. A huge dog.

"This is my baby, Velvet." Cathy knelt down to accept a lick on her cheek.

Yuk. Dog germs.

"Isn't he great?" she said. "He's just a puppy really—a chocolate lab. He won't hurt a flea. He just loves to give kisses, don't you, my Velvet? And he misses me when I'm at school and acts a little hyper. You still look freaked out, Julie. Don't you like dogs?"

"I'm allergic," I lied. It would have been more believable if I could have mustered up a sneeze. "I've never had a dog." It was much better than admitting most animals freaked me out.

"My room's the first door on the right. Go on in while I take Velvet out back. He'll be mad at me until later when I take him for his walk."

Cathy's room was painted blue with yellow moons and stars bordering the ceiling. A soft white canopy billowed from each corner of the bed.

"Wow," I told her when she came in. "Your room is great."

"Thanks." She closed the door. "My parents felt guilty about moving me to a new town, so they let me decorate my own room any way I wanted to."

"You did this yourself?"

"Mom helped. And I got a lot of ideas from those decorating shows on TV."

"I've never seen any. I don't watch much TV." My dad rarely bothered to hook it up when we moved.

"You don't watch decorating shows? It's a good thing you're my friend. It's on right now." We sat on the bed and watched her favorite show on a small TV. One team changed a crowded loft into a cool room for a teenager and by the time the show was over I wanted to redecorate my room. Actually, I wanted to redecorate my whole life.

After a delicious meal where I pretended I belonged in a family who ate at the table talking and laughing together like they did, Cathy walked me half way home in the dwindling light. It wasn't hard to keep my distance from Velvet who strained at the leash, practically pulling Cathy's arm out of the socket as he tried to run ahead and smell every fence post.

"I hate all the homework we have," Cathy said as she waved goodbye at the corner. "My mom's going to make me do it all before anything else, even though we have a three-day weekend." The speed of her talking had increased with the speed Velvet made her walk.

When I stepped into the house, I needed a little more of a welcome than I got from the family of cardboard boxes that lived near the door. Even Dad had to be better than nothing.

I expected to find him working on the different pieces that will make up his mural. But when I ran up the narrow attic steps I found him at a small easel I hadn't noticed before. The harsh lamp behind him highlighted the creases in his forehead. I stood in the doorway and rubbed at the stupid goosebumps popping up over my arms again. *Okay, Okay! So, what do YOU need?*

A fierce pain throbbed through my chest as a vision of Mom dying in the street flashed in my brain.

"What's wrong?" he looked up at my gasp and covered the canvas with a cloth.

"Nothing. I, uh, hit my elbow on the doorway," I thought it would look better if I actually rubbed my elbow—so I did. I would have to practice lying now that I was a freak. "I just came up to tell you I was back."

I rushed downstairs to the front porch and collapsed on the steps as I tried to stop panting.

"This isn't fair," I said to the empty street. "I just want to be normal. I want my own life back."

Forcing my heart to stop racing by slowing my breaths, I searched the streets for anyone witnessing another of my breakdowns. Beams from the crescent moon lighted dark rows of a hillside vineyard.

Sonoma wasn't such a bad little town to land in. Ringed by old buildings filled with restaurants and gift shops, the shady park sat in the town's center. It was the best place we'd landed in so far.

But I knew better than to become attached.

Maybe if I had a real life here, Dad would let me stay. *If I really am a Changer, why can't I get something I want?*

"You hear that?" I whispered to the moon. "I want to stay."

Chapter 8

Pink light filled the room when I opened my eyes. I knew it was early morning, but why was I standing next to my bed with both hands on the stack of boxes? My t-shirt was soaked in sweat and I shivered. *Gross. Wasn't Changing creepy enough? Did I have to start walking in my sleep?*

The dream was clear—a shining rainbow-colored triangle suspended between me and the ceiling. Mom was there, calling my name.

I heard knocking at the front door. I grabbed a sweatshirt and ran downstairs. *So much for sleeping in.* "Who is it?"

"Your landlord. I'm here to fix the garbage disposal."

I hurried to the door and let her in.

"Hi, Ms. Donovan," I said.

"You can call me Christine on weekends," she said. Dressed in jeans and a San Francisco Giants t-shirt, she looked more like a college student than my teacher. "Sorry I'm here so early. It's the only time I had. What are you up to?"

I followed her around the boxes and into the kitchen. "Nothing." *Just hanging out being a freak.*

"You guys haven't gotten around to unpacking yet, huh?"

"Only the important stuff. I never know from place to place if it's even okay to hang up a picture, so we usually just leave it packed."

"What about your room?" she asked as she turned on the disposal only to hear a grinding noise. "Which one did you choose?"

"The front one upstairs that looks on the street."

"That was my room, too," She opened the cabinet under the sink and stuck her head in. "When my aunt got sick, I transferred to Sonoma State University and lived here to help out. That's how I ended up with this house."

"Why don't you live here?"

"Too big for just me. I have a small condo. I always thought I'd have a family some day, but it hasn't worked out yet. The rental is good extra money. Most of the teachers here have some kind of second job." She pulled a small tool from her back pocket and ducked her head back under the sink. I heard a crunching sound. "You know you don't have to worry about this old house. She's seen a hundred years of pictures and she's still standing. Do whatever you want. There are so many layers of paint, one more wouldn't hurt."

"I can paint my room?"

"Sure. Just protect the hardwood floors while you're working, so I won't have any sanding to do next year. I hate to sand."

"This is so great!"

"What?" Dad asked as he entered the room. But I noticed his attention was on Ms. Donovan. Or to be exact, on her rear end. I tried to think of the gunky stuff trapped in the garbage disposal to keep from getting any of the details of his thoughts.

Ms. Donovan turned to wiggle out and caught him looking. She smiled. "I was just telling Julie she could paint her room." She ran the water in the sink and flicked the switch. The disposer hummed smoothly. "All done here."

"Thanks," Dad said. *Did his voice actually crack?*

"I know just the color I want to use." I was so excited I was even happy to see my dad.

"Why bother?" Dad asked.

"Because I've never been able to choose my room color before."

"Seems like a lot of work when we'll be moving again in a few months."

Oh yeah. That*'s why I feel crappy around him.* "Is it okay if I do it anyway?"

"Okay with me as long as you don't expect me to help."

I don't expect you to do anything.

He gave me his undivided attention. "Excuse me, young lady?"

"Uh, I mean Cathy's painted her room before, so she can help." I didn't want Ms. Donovan to see what a jerk my Dad was.

"So Drew," Ms. Donovan said, "I'm going to catch some breakfast around the corner. Would you care to join me?"

"I—uh—uh...." he stammered.

Real smooth Dad.

He turned and glared at me. "No. I can't. I have to work."

"Too bad," she shrugged her shoulders. "Let me know if you need anything else. See you at school, Julie."

I walked her to the door while Dad ran upstairs. *Chicken.*

Cathy and I walked to the hardware store and picked over the paint color chips for all of thirty seconds before I chose the right one—'Lucky Lavender.' I even liked the name. I waited in line while Cathy checked out desk organizers.

The gallon can didn't seem so heavy when we walked out of the store, but within a block it was tugging my arm out of its socket. The thin metal handle left marks on each of our hands as we took turns carrying it. By the time we reached home, I was cradling it in my arms.

"So..." When Cathy started out slow, I was afraid to find out which direction she was going in, "when are you going to tell me about Jason?"

"Jason?" The can almost slipped from my hands. I caught it before it landed on my foot. "I don't know what you mean…"

"Yeah, right. I've seen the way you look at him. It's like he's a super burrito and you've skipped lunch."

I tried to think up a lie, but I'd been covering up so much lately, I couldn't do it. "That obvious, huh?"

"Maybe not to everyone, but I pick things up pretty fast. So what are you going to do about it?"

"Nothing. I mean I think he's got a great smile and all, but he's taking Kelly to the Homecoming Dance. They're obviously a couple. She hangs on him whenever he's around."

"I heard that Kelly asked him to the dance. Their parents work together. They're practically brother and sister. And he may like you, too. You won't know until you ask."

"Well then I'll never know, because there's no way I'm going to ask."

"I could do it for you."

"Don't even think about it! I don't even want to talk about it anymore. Let's get to the painting."

We piled everything on my bed and pushed it into the middle of the room and covered it with tarps. In only two hours we had all four walls painted and Cathy had to go home to dinner. Two more hours later and I had the paint drips cleaned off the trim, the floor and my arms.

Lucky Lavender. Life felt better already.

"Yes!" I shouted to no one as I surveyed my room. A few spots I had missed popped out, but the thought of touch-ups didn't cut the thrill of having left my mark on my space, my home.

I still couldn't believe I was going to be able to make it the way I wanted it to be. I pulled the plastic drop cloths off the piled bed and pushed the pieces back into place, careful to miss the still tacky walls.

The tattered stack of boxes that I had woken up next to about twelve hours before called out for attention against my fresh walls.

Unopened and ignored for seven years, they stood as a reminder of the part of my life that hadn't been working—denial. My life needed more than a fresh coat of paint. Goosebumps covered my arms as I reached for the top box.

Chapter 9

Plastic Barbie shoes sprinkled my feet as I pulled the dry tape away and raised the cardboard flaps. Three worn dolls, each with their hair cut short, lay on top of a large bed of tiny dresses.

I picked one up, and rubbed the short hair. The day I'd chopped their hair off, I had decided to become a hairdresser. Apparently a punk stylist. Folding the flaps together to hold the box closed, I pulled a marker from my backpack and wrote, "Barbies—save for Julie." I placed the box near the door.

The next box was filled with tissue. My heart jumped as I unwrapped the first bundle. A delicate golden string that held a crystal shaped like a small crescent moon. I remembered this. *Mom.* The light traveled through the crystal, pulling out spots of color that danced against the wall the same way I remembered from her room. I set the piece aside, wiped a tear that had run down my cheek and opened the next bundle—a brass dolphin jumping over a crystal wave.

It was cool to the touch. But when I carried it past the window, a sudden heat covered my hands. I watched a pink color form on my palms and climb up my arms. When I turned my back to the light, the glow disappeared. *Bizarre how strange things are beginning to feel usual.*

I unwrapped the rest of the box—mostly ceramic animals and I placed them about the room, then hung the crescent moon in the window.

Soon I had opened every box in the room and hauled up the things I didn't need to the attic. Except for Mom's collection, most held my old toys. A large knot built in my throat. I had stopped playing the day Mom died. *How pathetic.*

"Moving back in?" Dad asked from the doorway. He hadn't seen my room yet. "Wow. It sure is purple." His gaze hit the crystal dolphin on the nightstand and he froze. The goosebumps started again.

"I unpacked my old boxes," I said. "I put some toys up in the attic. I suppose I should give some away."

"Marina's crystals." He was not listening.

I stopped breathing for a moment. It was the first time I'd heard him mention Mom's name in a long time. He picked up the dolphin with a shaky hand. His light mood swung quickly dark, like something switched off inside of him. My legs gave out and I collapsed on the bed. He returned the crystal to the nightstand and turned his back on it.

"It seems like you went to a lot of trouble when we'll be leaving in June."

I had been expecting this. It was no surprise, but it still stung. "I thought maybe you might like it here and want to stay a while longer."

"You know my work moves. I have to follow."

And drag me along.

"Do we have to do this now?" he snapped. "Or can you hold your sarcastic comments until tomorrow? I'm tired."

He walked out and my happiness drained away.

Reclining into my pillow, I stroked the crystal wave below the dolphin. What was it that changed his mood so quickly? This was only glass and brass.

It was hard to feel moody after Cathy arrived. She threw her pajama-stuffed pillowcase on the floor and plopped onto my bed.

She picked up a picture from the nightstand. "You look a lot like your mom. She was sure pretty."

"Thanks. That was taken just before she died."

Cathy put the picture down and then picked up the brass dolphin and walked to the window.

"This crystal looks so great with the sun coming in." She put the dolphin on the sill beneath the crescent moon. An immediate heat burned on my chest. The crystal from my necklace reflected light from the other two.

"Hey, they play off each other. Look at the pattern on the ceiling," Cathy said.

I leaned back on the bed. Light shone through the two crystals in the window and created rainbow-colored beams that met on the ceiling with a third ray connected to the crystal hanging from my necklace. The triangle of color began to darken into a swirling mist. "What is that?" I asked just as a clear picture emerged—Mom's face!

"Just the refraction from the crystals," Cathy said in her school voice. "Haven't you ever played with them before?"

I snatched the dolphin from the sill and fumbled for words. "Oh, uh, I mean, sure. I just haven't seen it form that triangle before. Cool, huh? Say, thanks for staying with me tonight. I know you could have gone to the Homecoming Dance."

"Not without my best friend! But I still think you should have gone and asked Jason to dance."

"That would have gone over great with Kelly. Besides, he probably would have said no. Let's go downstairs and find something to eat. It's too smelly to stay in here tonight anyway."

I tried not to think of Jason dancing with Kelly. I was also trying not to think of the crystals. So when we set up camp in the living room, I was totally thinking of both Jason and the crystals. When Cathy went into the bathroom, I ran back up to my room.

But the sun had moved away from the window. Whatever secrets the crystals held would have to wait.

Chapter 10

Dolores picked up Cathy after lunch for a Sunday drive—whatever that was. A break in the clouds caused an explosion of sunlight through the living room windows as I closed the front door.

"Here goes nothing." Tip-toeing up the stairs, I peeked into my room like I was afraid of finding a mouse running across the floor. Immediately the warmth of my necklace spread across my chest and pulled me forward to the other crystals.

The same triangle of light met on the ceiling and began to swirl as I sat on my bed and watched. I was shaking, but I wasn't cold—I was scared.

The center of the light became dark and murky. Inside the swirling mist I glimpsed an image, small at first and then large and clear.

Mom carried a birthday cake to a table. Candle glow sparkled in her smiling eyes. From the familiar chocolate creation I knew that it was my birthday. Nine candles. My last birthday with Mom.

The smell of melting wax and sweet frosting filled my nose as I watched my young self blow out the candles. Dad, his hair a mass of shoulder-length curls, smiled widely without a crease on his smooth face.   Mom looked as she did in most pictures, with her straight brown hair pulled back into a clip. Gramma was there too, but her brown hair held no hint of gray. "Happy Birthday to you," they sang in unison and off key.

After I opened my presents—the blonde Barbie with the pink plastic molded bed set, a white My Little Pony with purple stars on its back, and an Easy Bake oven— Mom began to speak.

"It's time to give our wishes to Julie. Mom, you can go first."

"I wish you a year of love and happiness," Gramma said.

"I wish you another great year at school. Keep up the good work," Dad said.

"What's your wish dear?" Gramma asked Mom.

"Well, I keep thinking of my own wish," Mom continued, "that time would freeze and I could keep things just as they are, here with those I love the most." Her voice choked and a tear rolled down her cheek. Dad rose and put an arm around her shoulder. "Since I know I can't stop time, I'll wish that you will always be able to remember this happiness of us here, together, as we are right now. I love you, Jewel Anne."

Mom hugged me and then Dad hugged us both. I felt warmth and comfort sandwiched between my parents. When the vision faded away it was like I was falling through a dark hole.

"Mom," I whimpered, then dropped into a deep sleep where the vision I'd seen played over and over, always ending with the hug.

A hand on my shoulder woke me.

"Julie?" I jumped awake, my head aching. It was nearly black in my room, the only light coming from the hallway. Dad stood over me in a dark silhouette. "Oh, I didn't know you were asleep. I was going to ask you to go to the store for coffee. Guess I'll go myself."

"Okay." I sat up as he left the room, my head instantly pounding. "You could have asked me if I wanted anything!" And I could have used a number of things.

The clock and the darkened room said I'd slept all afternoon.

I picked up the crystal dolphin and the crescent moon. Crystals just like these were sold in shops right on the Plaza. They didn't look special, but they sure knocked me out.

The brass dolphin looked as if it had just jumped from the water and was now pointed nose-down ready to dive back in. The nose balanced onto a small brass plate, engraved with ripples. Turning it over, I read the writing on the bottom: "Beulah N.O. 1973."

When I heard the front door close I grabbed the phone to call Gramma. I was a little afraid. So far all of the strange things she had told me had come true. I didn't really want to know if there was more. But I had to find out about the crystals.

Gramma answered on the first ring. "What's up, honey?"

"My fricken' legacy—that's what's happened." I said. "How much do you know about Mom's crystals?"

"They were birthday gifts. Why?"

"They created a vision like a lightshow on my ceiling, showing home movies of my past," I explained the vision. "Did you know they did that? I could smell the cake. I could feel the hug. It was the most bizarre home movie I've ever seen."

"My goodness! Let me see," Gramma said. "The crystals were a gift from Beulah. She was an old friend of my mother's, and Rose's too. I haven't seen her in years."

"How could you not know about the crystals? I mean, you knew Beulah made them."

"I told you that your mom was a private person. Beulah knew that, too. She wouldn't have said anything to me if Marina hadn't wanted her to."

"Can we call Beulah? She'd probably tell us now."

"If I can track her down. She must be close to a hundred years old. She lived out in the bayou her whole life. I don't think she ever had a phone. I'll have to ask Rose what she knows. Oh, Jewel, this is so exciting."

"Yeah, right." I tried to rub the rest of the headache out of my forehead. I don't think I ever had a headache before I had powers. *This is far worse than puberty.* "I have no privacy in my own mind, and now I'm seeing faces in crystal. What's next?"

"You've already gone way past anything I'd expected," Gramma said. "I have no clue how far this will take you."

"Why did I know you were going to say something like that? By the way, it's not comforting."

Chapter 11

I stuck a wart on the end of Cathy's nose.

"Are you sure you don't want to be a witch, too?" Cathy asked me for the tenth time since she'd hauled her stuff over today.

"Positive." The last weeks of my crap had caused enough attention. No way was I going to wear a costume and trick-or-treat. Especially not a black hat and cape.

"Thanks for helping me get ready." Cathy twirled in her long skirt, spinning on our kitchen floor until her black boots caught where Dad had spilled the orange juice this morning. "I can't believe you don't like to dress up."

"It's just never been a big deal," I lied. Again. Mom and I had loved Halloween and always went all out on costumes. But no one needed to know how pitiful I really was.

I'd spent several afternoons with the crystals where I watched random visions of my childhood; including the Halloween when she dressed us both up as rag dolls. All I could think about was when Gramma finds Beulah. I couldn't figure out how these little memories were going to help me.

The doorbell rang and I ran for the bowl of candy. Two little girls, twins I thought, dressed as fairies, one in pink and one in blue, held out tiny plastic pumpkins.

"Oh, you are both so cute you're going to get loads of candy!" Cathy said. The girls stared at the green makeup I'd help smooth over Cathy's face. The lower lip of the pink fairy started to quiver. I dumped most of the bowl into the totes and pulled Cathy back inside.

"Why don't you let them get a head start before you go to Thomas'? I think they're a little scared of your costume."

The doorbell rang again and I opened the door to face Kelly, standing in front of a group of three of her posse. I didn't know what to say.

She did. Dressed as a French maid, her already large breasts looked enormous and jiggled side to side as she laughed. At me. "Nice costume," she said.

I tugged self-consciously at my t-shirt then realized she was staring at my crystal necklace. I covered it with my hand.

"What are you going as?" she asked. "A loser?"

Ignore her! I reached out to drop candy into their pillowcases when Kelly pulled hers back.

"That's okay," Kelly said. "You keep your candy. It's nothing like the good stuff my mom's giving out anyway." She was lying. I knew her parents were gone for the weekend. I knew because I'd heard her moping about it all week.

Cathy pressed against my back like she wanted through me to get at Kelly. I pushed back. But I was getting tired of my 'just let it go' motto.

Kelly took in Cathy's hair, carefully frizzed out from under her pointed black hat. "Could you possibly be any uglier?" Kelly asked as she flicked her long straight hair behind her shoulder.

Cathy's eyes narrowed and she stepped around me, now face to face with Kelly. "Why thank you," Cathy said. "I am a witch, you know. And what are you?" Cathy slowly looked from Kelly's water-filled breasts to her fish-net stockings. "Oh yeah. You're a sl-"

I grabbed her arm with one hand and put one finger on her mouth.

"Aren't you leaving?" I asked Cathy.

"I sure am," Cathy said, staring down Kelly until she cleared the doorway and waved goodbye. Kelly followed her to the sidewalk and stopped when Kevin called from across the street.

"Hey Kelly, it's time!" Kevin said.

I tried to eavesdrop from the porch as I pretended to check the candle on the battery-powered pumpkin. It was a warm night. The end of Indian summer. Why do they call it that? I get Russian winters and Paris in the spring, but wouldn't Arizona summers better describe a last blast of heat before winter comes?

Someone laughed. Not the kind of laugh like someone just told a funny joke. The kind of laugh that said something that shouldn't happen was about to.

They huddled together at the edge of the lawn. What were they saying? Oh yeah, duh! I could find out.

What are you planning Kelly?

Kelly pulled the shoulder straps of her costume to adjust her water boobs. *This is going to be great. That witch won't ever know what hit her until she's completely soaked.*

Cathy! I left the candy on the porch and ran for the phone. But after I dialed Cathy's number a phone rang behind me. Cathy had left her cell phone on the couch! Back on the porch I picked up the bowl and pretended not to pay attention to Kelly.

Eddie walked up the sidewalk and turned at my house when he saw me. Apparently he'd decided to dress as up as an ex-athlete turned possible drug-using teenager with family problems. No costume. Just a trick-o-treat bag. He gave that little head bob that guys do instead of waving and came up to the door.

"Hey," he said.

I didn't have time to deal with his problems or worry about what he might think of me. "Have you seen Cathy? She's on her way to Thomas'."

"No. What's up?"

A new batch of ninjas came up the walk and I waited to say anything until they were gone.

"Kelly," I whispered. "She's planning on nailing someone with those water balloons she's hauling around. I want to make sure it's not Cathy, but she left her phone here, so I can't warn her."

"That's a no-brainer," Eddie said. "Go tell Kelly to leave Cathy alone!"

"Are you kidding? She already hates my guts. She'll beat the crap out of me."

Eddie rolled his eyes. "You really are a wuss."

"Thanks!" I tried to look put out, but he was right. "She's always making life crappy for someone. I wish something would happen to her for a change."

Kelly laughed and anger grew inside me and spread into a rash over my arms. *She makes me so mad!*

A scream pierced the air. It was Kelly. Even from my porch, it was easy to see the large wet stains and Kelly's shocked face. The balloons tucked into her costume had burst.

"Whoa! Wish granted." Eddie grabbed the last of the candy and headed back down the steps.

"Yeah, right," I squeaked and slammed the door. I sunk to a heap on the floor.

There's no way I did that! But... The empty bowl stared back at me. "I wish this was still full of candy." Nothing. I sighed and shook my head. "This power crap has got me believing anything's possible."

But I was sure of one thing. I was tired of being a wuss. Maybe I could learn how to stand up for myself. Fight back. How, I wasn't sure yet, but I'd do something. Of course, if no one knew it was me, that would be better. If I had real powers I could be a superhero. Anonymous of course.

Chapter 12

I stirred cut-up hot dogs into the macaroni and cheese and an orange-coated blob plopped onto the green-tiled counter.

"Five-second rule." I scooped it up and popped it into my mouth. "Hot-Hot!" But good-good.

My life sucks, so I thought I'd try for a small change for me. My plan, well more like my hope, was to try using good to bring Dad around like when Gramma was here. I'd even set the table with plates and napkins. When he comes down to eat, we might just talk.

At the bottom of the attic stairs I called out "dinner." No answer. No surprise. I climbed up the last steps and looked into the studio. Although he had complained of being behind in his work, Dad was not standing at the large mural canvas. He sat near the window facing the small easel. Light filtered past a new batch of clouds and left shadows on his pain face. I stayed hidden in the hallway.

Goosebumps started at my ankles and traveled upward. When they reached my throat, they built into a large lump, which exploded into a question that gave me away. *What's the matter?*

It's all wrong. Dad's thoughts blared. *Why can't I remember?*

"I made dinner," I croaked, not ready for his strong feelings. He looked over the top of the easel, his eyes dark and unreadable. "It's going to cool off."

"Later," he mumbled.

I wanted to leave, but he needed help. "What are you working on?" I forced my feet to walk across the room.

He pulled a cloth over the canvas. "Can't I have some privacy in my own studio?"

Ouch. "Sorry." *Why did I want to have dinner with him?* He bent back over his work as the phone rang.

I hurried downstairs and was relieved to hear Cathy's voice. "Hey, Mom just invited you for dinner. Did you already eat?"

My one-pot masterpiece didn't look as special as it had before Dad started growling. "Nope. I'll be right over."

Meandering my way to Cathy's I enjoyed being outside. The rows of grapevines that covered the hills around me looked so different now. All of the golden leaves had dropped, leaving the valley surrounded in brown wooden stripes. And no one was around to hide my thoughts from.

Cathy's front lawn was the only one of the block not covered in leaves. Her dad had turned raking into his new job. I rang the doorbell and waited.

Dolores opened the door and shook her head at me. "What are you doing ringing the bell?"

"Oh, uh...should I have knocked?"

"No, silly. You're family now. Just come on in." She pulled me into a hug. *Wow.* Maybe she could officially adopt me.

Cathy and I set the table and helped bring the food to the table. The big tray of fried chicken and bowls of mashed potatoes and vegetables sure looked like a lot for four people.

Dinner tasted so fresh. Not like what I usually micro waved. I shoveled a second helping of mashed potatoes onto my plate. "These are great," I said. "They actually taste like real potatoes."

"Thank you," Dolores laughed. "I've been meaning to ask if you and your father would like to come over for Thanksgiving dinner. Your grandmother won't be here and I hate to think of the two of you eating alone on the holiday."

"That'd be great, Julie!" Cathy said. "We'd have so much fun and I wouldn't have to just hang around my brothers all day."

Being alone on Thanksgiving would suck. But Dad hadn't been much on polite conversation for a while. It would be so embarrassing to have him grunt his way through dinner.

"Thanks." I tried to think up an excuse. "But we have plans."

"Oh good. What are you going to do?"

"Uh, well, um... we always get up early and put the turkey in the oven, then, uh, we hang out and watch the parades on TV...uh... and maybe this year we're thinking of helping serve dinner to the needy."

"That sounds wonderful," Dolores said. "We'll miss you, but I'm so glad you two have such a nice plan."

Where did feed the needy come from? It was difficult to swallow the rest of my dinner past the lies caught in my throat.

When Dolores drove me home later, I didn't want to get out of the car. But after Cathy said goodbye twice and I was still buckled, it grew awkward, so I got out.

"I'm back," I announced from the studio doorway.

"Hmm," Dad grunted. His attention never left the easel.

"You know, because I was at Cathy's for dinner."

He held the paintbrush in his teeth for a moment and stood back to frown at the painting. "Uh-huh," he grunted again.

"See ya." I hadn't heard a real word from him in days. It would be funny if it wasn't so sad.

After cleaning up the untouched macaroni and cheese, I stuffed the last of the laundry into the washing machine. By the time the clothes were dried, folded, and put away and my homework finished, I crawled exhausted under the covers. Dad's footsteps paced across the floor above me.

"All that work and he never came down to eat." I pounded my backpack into submission. Okay, I hit it once. It was a bad idea. My knuckles were sore and I broke both of the pencils in the front pocket. Maybe I should have let Gramma talk to him about sharing the chores.

He's still the same, but I'm different. If I do something for him, I want him to appreciate it. Since he can't...Forget Plan A. I'll think of something else. In the meantime, he can take care of himself!

Chapter 13

Wearing pillow wrinkles on his cheek, Eddie passed my desk in English ten minutes after class had started. I wanted to pay attention to Ms. Donovan. I wanted to go home sick. I wanted to do anything else, but the frown on Eddie's face, drew my thoughts into his.

Helping him had to be easier than Dad. *What's wrong, Eddie?*

His thoughts were sharp and angry. *I should have stayed home. At least she was finally sleeping. When was the last time I slept through the night? Oh yeah. Before that jerk ran out on us.*

"Hello, Julie. Can you pay attention to class now?" Ms. Donovan asked. *How long had she been standing right next to me?*

The entire class turned to face my—I was sure—red face. "Uh, yeah."

"Nice to have your attention back."

Helping Eddie was going to have to happen outside of class. But where?

After school, I saw him walking about a half a block ahead. When he turned the corner, I knew what I had to do. I glanced around—not really sure what I was looking for—and followed him. He crossed another street and then headed toward the Plaza. Past a restaurant and a wine shop, he turned down an alley I hadn't explored.

"I should have known there'd be an alley involved." It felt like every movie I had seen where someone is followed into a dark dirty alley—although this one was bright and incredibly clean. Hopefully this would be one of the movies where something funny would happen, not one about a serial killer who lured people behind dumpsters.

The alley opened into a small courtyard with a Mexican restaurant and several small shops. I hid behind a sandwich board advertising daily specials when he walked into a chocolate shop. *How did I miss that store?*

He came out with a small bag and I followed him to the back of the courtyard where he cut through a parking lot. I dashed behind tree to tree for two blocks. I was about as stealth as a squirrel, if the squirrel was carrying an enormous backpack full of nuts. Eddie turned right and crossed into a neighborhood of large new homes.

Although only blocks from the tiny rows of houses in town, Eddie's house had a long front porch complete with several rocking chairs like an old farm house built one hundred years ago. A thin woman, her head wrapped in a scarf, sat in a rocking chair. I stopped to pretend to tie my shoe, and then realized that wouldn't work. Darn flip flops! I ducked behind a huge tree with bright red and green leaves that seemed unable to make up its mind whether it was summer or fall.

"Hi Mom," Eddie said, his normally slurred voice sounding sober. "How are you feeling?"

"Better," she said. "It was a good day."

"I wish you'd hire someone to be here when I'm at school."

"There's no need. I'm fine."

"Did you at least eat today?" He tucked a blanket in around his mother's lap. "I bought some of the chocolates you like—and maybe some tea?"

"You're trying to fatten me up," she said, with a weak laugh. "Actually, I'm not very hungry. Maybe later."

"Mom, you know you need to eat."

"Oh, Edward." She closed her eyes and rocked back in the chair. "Just let me enjoy this sunshine for a little longer, then I promise I'll come in and eat something."

"All right, Mom," he said as he opened the front door. "I'll start dinner."

Eddie's mom closed her eyes and rocked back and forth. Like some creepy stalker, I couldn't tear my eyes away. Her face was so peaceful soaking in the warm sunshine.

Meow! I jumped and scratched my elbow on the tree as a fat barrel-shaped cat rubbed up against my legs.

Without checking to see if I'd been spotted, I hurried away.

The late afternoon sun was setting into a bank of black clouds on the horizon. Squinting made my eyes water. But when I crossed the street to walk in the shade of the tree-lined sidewalk, a tear slipped down my cheek. Eddie's mom was sick. Maybe dying. But still I wished I were Eddie. I wanted Mom. Even if it was only for a little while more.

A stack of Dad's dishes in the sink greeted me when I walked into the kitchen. At Cathy's house everyone helped keep things clean. But they were a family. We were just roommates. I left the mess.

Chapter 14

Thanksgiving morning I stood by the dryer to keep reshutting the door when my tennis shoes hit it open. I couldn't take the embarrassing squeaking noises they made through the school hallways during this week's rainstorm. Plus soggy socks suck.

"Good, you're finally cleaning this up," Dad said as he walked into the kitchen. He opened then quickly slammed the refrigerator door. "And there's nothing to eat in this house. There's not even a can of soup left. And look at these dishes all over the counter."

"Don't look at me." I pulled out one shoe and checked the inside for dampness. "This is your mess."

"This can't be all me." He waved to the dirty stack. "I'm hungry and even if we had a stinking can of soup in this house, I wouldn't have a clean bowl. And look at that laundry pile. This has to change."

Stepping over piles of his laundry with my bare feet, I loaded my jacket into the dryer, still wet from yesterday. I tried hard not to react to his tantrum and struggled to keep my mind clear. I wouldn't back down. His mess was his. Period.

I grabbed my shoes and headed for the door. Raining or not, I was outta there! *I hope that he'll have his crap cleaned up before I get back.*

"My crap? Wait one minute, young lady. We're not through here." He took a step forward and nearly slipped on one of his dirty socks. He kicked it fiercely.

Oh, great. "Through with what?"

"This. . . this *mess*. What's going on with you lately? All this backtalk you've been giving me and now this catastrophe."

"Backtalk?" I answered slowly. I'd wanted to keep my voice calm so I could leave but his face looked so angry I cracked. "Doesn't there have to be "first talk" before there can be backtalk?"

"What?"

I'm so over worrying about his precious feelings! "You never talk to me except to ask me to do something for you: find my shoes, iron my shirt, heat up some soup." The words exploded out so fast even I was surprised. "Do you even know me? And, for the record, every one of these dishes and every piece of that laundry pile belongs to you. I keep my own things clean."

I stood up straight, but I shook inside and waited for his reaction.

"You never used to mind."

He was right. I never did. *But now it's different. Everything is different. Except maybe him. He hasn't changed in seven years.*

"There! That's exactly what I'm talking about." He raised both his hands, like he couldn't believe the weight he had to balance on them. "You used to be such a sweet, easy-going girl."

That's it? Didn't he care? "What about what I just said?"

"Let's drop it. I'll clean this mess up and you can go to the store."

I pointed at the window where the wind was now blowing a new batch of raindrops sideways against the pane. "That might be a little difficult."

He pinched his lips together then bit out, "Okay. I'll drive."

The inside of our car was as silent as Miss Day's classroom when she asks someone to explain photosynthesis.

I pushed my cart to the open door just as Eddie pushed his cart out.

"Hey," he said. He wore a black t-shirt with a large picture of some band I didn't recognize and his hair hung in greasy clumps. He looked like one of the piles of laundry I'd just left at home.

"Hey. What's up?" Did he know I'd followed him?

"Nothing." The bags in Eddie's cart were filled with the same type of instant food I planned to buy. His Thanksgiving would be as crappy as mine.

"Who's this?" Dad asked. I'd forgotten he was there.

"This is Eddie. He's in my English class."

Dad nodded but did not smile. "Hello."

"Hey." Eddie looked at Dad's face and pulled his cart out of the doorway. Obviously this wasn't a good first impression for either of them. "I gotta go."

Dad didn't say a word until Eddie was gone and we were on the second aisle.

"That kid isn't one of your close friends, is he?"

"No," I said. We weren't really *friends*, but I'd have to say we were close since I could read his frickin' mind. "Just someone I know from school, why?"

"I didn't like the looks of him. I don't want you hanging around stoners."

I threw a can of green beans in and winced when it sounded like the jar of mayonnaise may have cracked. "He's not that bad when you get to know him."

"Having friends like him would explain a lot about your issues—about the changes you seem to be going through."

"I don't have issues," I whined. Okay, that was a lie, but he didn't know about my powers. "And you shouldn't judge Eddie just by his clothes. He's going through a lot with his mother. She's real sick."

Dad shook his head. "It's guys like him that make me glad we keep moving."

Now he wanted to play Dad? I didn't sign up for this gig and I couldn't quit if I wanted to. And I really wanted to.

I groaned when I saw the long check out lines. Dad groaned louder. He decided to wait in the car. With all the last-minute holiday shoppers, even the shortest line looked about a mile long.

While I inched forward I eavesdropped on the other shoppers. They were all talking about dressing recipes, football, and relatives waiting at home. For a while, I let myself pretend my holiday wasn't so pitiful. Then I heard a familiar voice.

"I can't believe I forgot the rolls again." *Dolores!* She was in the next aisle, on the opposite side of a Cheerios display, talking to another shopper. "Every year I either forget to buy them, or forget to put them in the oven."

She can't see me! Not after all that crap I made up about my family Thanksgiving. The line began to move again and my heart raced.

"You go ahead of me," I said to the elderly couple behind me. "I, uh, forgot something." I pulled a box of macaroni and cheese off the shelf and began reading the back. Like I didn't have the recipe memorized: ¼ cup margarine, ¼ cup milk, one lonely life.

I waved four more carts through and twenty more minutes by before taking my place back in line. Dolores was gone. The coast was clear.

Home alone. Again. I warmed up my microwave dinner and then spooned it out of the small compartments onto a real plate. If I'd known before that it wouldn't have made a difference no matter what I said to Dad, I wouldn't have bit my tongue for so long. I lighted the candle in the shape of a pilgrim I'd found in the half-off bin at the store.

Turning on the TV to a replay of the morning's Thanksgiving Day parade I sat down and imagined my life differently. Now I was like the large floating animals I was watching on TV. They wanted to fly up and away, but the wind batted them side to side and the strings held them to the ground.

Chapter 15

Toasting Christmas vacation with one-liter bottles of root beer, Cathy celebrated no homework for two weeks. I raised my sticky bottle of fizz to freedom from Kelly and Eddie's thoughts.

"Thank God I didn't have to go shopping with my parents again," Cathy flopped back on the couch. "It's not like they take my advice on what to buy my brothers."

"Maybe that's because you suggested buying your brother Jeff a boa constrictor."

"I still think that's a great idea—his apartment has rats!" Cathy stretched and leaned back against the pillow, staring at her now growing breasts. "But I do need to go bra shopping. These puppies are finally busting out."

"I don't want to know." I lifted a stack of newspaper off a moving box and found the remote control.

"You're just jealous."

"You're right." I don't mind my small boobs. What I'm jealous about is that she has time to worry about something so utterly personal when I had to worry about everyone else.

"I know you guys like to have these boxes stacked around," Cathy said, "but where are you going to put your Christmas tree?"

"We don't put up a tree," I said. That's for normal families.

"You're kidding. Oh—I never asked, are you Jewish or something? I mean that's cool."

"Nope. We used to put up a tree when I was little, but we haven't since we left New Orleans."

"Not in seven years?" Cathy said. "I can't believe it. I mean Christmas without a tree! We go to the mountains every year with the whole family to pick out our tree. Mom decorates it the week after Thanksgiving and we keep it up until New Year's Eve. The needles are usually falling off and Dad won't turn on the lights past Christmas because he says it's a fire hazard."

"I think it reminds my father of when my mom was killed. It was the week before Christmas. Our tree stayed up until January before Gramma finally took it down." *Oh no! Today is the anniversary. No wonder Dad's been acting extra weird—* Wait...I've never forgotten the date before. *Is this good because it means I'm moving on? Or that I'm a bad daughter?*

"That so sucks," Cathy said. "I can't imagine Christmas without a tree, let alone without my mom. Maybe you should ask your dad—I mean, if you want one."

Did I want a tree? I hadn't really thought about it, but yeah, I did want a tree. And lights and decorations and gifts, too. Sorta. "I'm not sure Dad is ready," I said.

"Let's ask Gramma Aurora, she'll know what to do." Cathy was already up and heading for the guest room. Gramma had arrived late last night. I'd wanted to ask her about the crystals and if she found out anything from Beulah when she arrived last night, but she just said to be patient. *Does she even know me?*

Gramma liked the tree idea and minutes later they were both pushing me into the studio.

Dad looked up from his work. "This looks like an official visit."

"Well, uh," I stammered. "I, we were talking about it and thought maybe we should have a Christmas tree this year. Maybe."

His smile faded and I could feel a pain well up in him—in both of us.

"But if you don't want to, it's okay," I blurted, then turned to the door.

"I'd help." Cathy turned me back around. *Traitor!*

"Me, too," Gramma said. "It's about time Christmas was celebrated by this family again."

Dad's face looked like he had just stubbed his toe. "I guess I'm outvoted. Just don't ask me to help. I don't have time to drive around looking for some tree that will just have to be taken down in a week. I can't imagine where you could find the space to put it, anyway. "

"I'll move some boxes and I'll get a little tree," I said. "I could put it up myself and I'll take it down too."

"Go ahead." His attention turned back to his drawing board. It wasn't exactly the Christmas cheer I had been hoping for, but at least he'd agreed.

The tree I picked out at the grocery store an hour later wouldn't fit into Gramma's rental car. Cathy and I decided to carry it home while Gramma finished shopping.

Bundled in my despised Seattle rain gear, I carried the tree by the wooden stand nailed to the bottom while Cathy held on to the tip.

"Step here, oops, I mean step now," Cathy had to give directions as we tried to navigate the crosswalk. "Oh! Hi, Eddie."

I peeked around the branches at Eddie. That guy turned up everywhere.

"Seems like a lot of work for one day," he said.

Great. Another Scrooge. "That's what my dad said. But we talked him into letting us put one up this year," I said.

"Want some help?"

"No. We got it. But thanks."

After Eddie was out of earshot, Cathy started in. "I'm trying to be nice, but he sure is odd. And I think he likes you. I know these things."

"Vibes? No way. *I* know these things," I said. I was uncomfortable talking about Eddie with Cathy, but I wasn't about to tell her that I could hear him think. I changed the subject. "This is an awesome tree!"

The last steps up to the porch were the hardest. We dragged the tree through the front door and set it up so it could be seen from the front window.

"You're going to need a stand with a bowl for water." Cathy stood back to admire the tree.

"I'm sure we have one somewhere." I waved at the tall stack of boxes we'd just moved into the hallway.

"Why is someone else's stuff always more fun to work on than your own?" Cathy asked, eagerly tearing into the mound. We sorted through the pile and pulled out those marked "X-Mas." "Eight boxes of Christmas! Wow. For a family that doesn't celebrate, you have a lot of stuff."

Cathy started a classic rock remix, turned up the volume on the CD player, and began digging deep. "Oh my God, this is like a treasure hunt. Do you have any lights? We have to put those on before the ornaments, but you have to test them first."

Once we strung about eight strands around our tree, we found out the one in the middle didn't work, so we had to take it apart.

Soon the tree branches were pointing to the ground under the weight of the decorations.

Gramma came in the front door and placed her shopping bags on the floor. "Oh, girls! That looks so good. Your mother would be so happy, Jewel. She loved Christmas."

It felt so good to hear that, I gave Gramma a big hug.

"I don't know," Cathy said, "there's something missing. It doesn't seem to blend in with the room. As long as we've opened this many boxes, why don't we get the rest out of the living room and stack them in the hall. We can cover the ones we can't empty with sheets and make tables like on the TV shows. Then we can take the decorations out of the rest."

Dad's gonna hate this idea. "Let's do it!"

We unpacked several books into the shelves surrounding the fireplace, placed a small nativity set on the mantle, and spread a garland and other Christmas knickknacks around the room. After we managed to squeeze a few more boxes into the closet under the stairs, we spent half an hour carrying empty boxes to the storage beneath the attic stairs.

We met on the landing. "Now this part seems like a lot of work for nothing," I huffed.

"I know, but Mom always makes us put the empty boxes away so we don't look at them during the holidays—like the Christmas stuff is up all year. Besides, you'd trip over them. Here's the last box. I thought it was empty, but there are gift boxes inside. My mom sometimes puts fake gifts under the tree before Christmas for decorations, too. I think it's dumb, so I brought the box up. You figure it out. I'm going to run to the bathroom and wash the sap off my elbow."

Three packages were wrapped in holiday paper. I set the box down and pulled them out. Goosebumps prickled up my arm as I touched the first package labeled 'Julie.' The other two read "Drew" and "Mom." I lifted mine out and shook it.

It wasn't empty.

Chapter 16

"Come on down here this minute Drew," Gramma called from the foot of the stairs after he had ignored her twice. "We're all going to the Plaza to hear the carolers. No more work tonight."

"You know, Aurora," Dad said when he appeared on the landing and pulled on his jacket. "Sometimes you sound just like my mom."

"Well, I feel like your mom sometimes, too, God rest her soul."

'Oh Come all Ye Faithful' could be heard before we crossed the street to the Plaza. It was a good thing because the sound took up the awkwardness of how quiet we were. Tonight was a big deal. It was the first holiday we'd acknowledged since Mom died. We had a tree and Gramma insisted we join in the town's Christmas Eve celebration. Just like a normal family. On the outside, at least.

Bundled in our warmest clothes and all wearing one of the many scarves I'd crocheted in Seattle last year, we sat on wooden benches that overlooked an outdoor stage.

Gramma unfolded a lap blanket over our laps. "Do you want some?" she asked Dad. "Drew?"

"Huh?" he said, clearly not looking at us, but at Ms. Donovan who had just walked up wearing a fitted red sweater dress, black tights and boots carrying a basket of candy canes.

"Merry Christmas," Ms. Donovan smiled, holding out a treat. "Care for something sweet?"

"N-n-no!" Dad stammered and knew then who I inherited my ability to blush Christmas red from. *How did he ever end up with Mom?*

"I still have a rain check on that lunch, right?" she said while handing me a candy cane.

"Uh, oh, well I don't get out much."

"That's an understatement," Gramma joined in. "I'm Aurora. Julie's grandmother."

"She's my English teacher and our landlady," I added.

"Nice to meet you. I'd better get back to work."

Dad watched her walk away and kept an eye on her as she mingled from family to family as Santa's helper.

Sucking on candy canes and pointing at the stage, three small kids stood on the bench next to me. Their parents were holding hands and they all sang loudly as they geared up for the big guy. Half an hour later when the carolers started "Here Comes Santa Claus," the kids went ballistic.

An elf began handing out small gifts to the kids. I'd stuffed the gifts Cathy had found under my bed. I'd been afraid of Dad's reaction. He'd already gone from his usual sad little boy self to a cranky Dad in the past two months. I didn't know where these gifts would take him. I was saving them for the morning when he couldn't get away.

Santa arrived in a decorated trolley car normally used to drive wine tasters around the valley. *How could we have skipped Christmas for seven years?*

"I was thinking, Drew," Gramma said on the short but crisp walk home, "I have to make a quick trip back to New Orleans—just two nights. It would be great if Julie could come along. What do you think?"

"Really?" I jumped in front of both of them and blocked the sidewalk. "Can I go, please?"

"That's a long flight for a couple of days," he said. "But I guess so. What do you plan to do?"

"Rose is gone for the month to her sister-in-law's and some issues have come up. It shouldn't take me long and then Julie and I can meet some old family friends."

She'd found Beulah!

"We can eat beignets for breakfast and crawfish for dinner," Gramma continued. "Maybe even an alligator steak."

"Yuk! Do we have to eat alligator?"

"My dear, it's a delicacy." Gramma blew a kiss from her gloved fingertips, drawing a rare smile from Dad.

"I'll take your word for it. Besides, I had a pact with all carnivores, particularly sharks and alligators–I wouldn't eat them if they didn't eat me."

Gramma told me tales of her friends and favorite places in New Orleans until late that night. The only memories I had of New Orleans were of Mom. Like one Christmas Eve when I was too excited to sleep and Mom let me stay up with her and watch for Santa Claus. She had turned out all the lights but the tree and let me snuggle under a blanket next to her. The only rule was, she said I couldn't say a word. But I could stay up as long as I wanted. I don't remember anything after that. Just the feeling of her hand softly rubbing my back as I lay on her lap watching the tree.

Chapter 17

A bright light woke me early Christmas morning. I was lying on my back as I opened my eyes and saw a rainbow swirling on the ceiling. The first rays of dawn had slid through the window and found the crystals. My heart raced. Jumping from sleep to vision wasn't my idea of a relaxing morning.

The vision materialized and it got worse. The day Mom had died.

We were leaving the park. At the first corner Mom reached for my hand. "I'm a big girl," I said, pulling away. "I don't need to hold my mom's hand to cross a street."

Mom leaned over and spoke in a calm but stern voice. "As far as I'm concerned, Jewel Anne, you will never be too old to hold my hand."

I gave in, sulking that I wasn't the boss and staring at my feet as we walked into the street.

"Not you!" Mom cried. Before I understood what was happening, pain tore at my arm. Brakes squealed and glass shattered around me like painful sparkling rain. Then I was lying next to the curb, my knees and hands scraped and bleeding. I never looked at the car. My eyes were on her.

"Mom!" I dragged myself up and ran around the car. She was lying on her back, her eyes open. The car screeched away. I knelt on wounded knees and held Mom's hand.

"Mommy, are you okay?"

"You're okay. Thank God." Mom let out a sigh, then coughed wetly. "I need to tell you," she huffed. "I thought I'd have more time. I've tried to save you from…I need to tell you…I can't believe it was her."

"Who?

A blaring siren of the ambulance drowned out her last cough. A female officer pulled me away, led me into a patrol car. Dad arrived just as they lifted a cloth-covered gurney into the ambulance. He ran crying to me, and held me so tight that I thought I might break from the inside out.

Chapter 18

The second time I woke up on Christmas morning the sun was up and the fierce pain from the accidental vision had lifted from my chest. Reliving the details of her death was not what I wanted to do. I picked up Mom's picture from my side table and wished her a Merry Christmas before running upstairs.

Stopping at Dad's door, I tapped softly. No answer. I knocked louder, then opened the door. The bed did not look like it had been slept in. No way would Dad make his bed this early.

No big guess where to find him. I peeked inside the studio door, expecting to find him asleep in front of one of the three murals he'd started. But as I stepped inside he was working furiously at the small easel.

Knowing the pain was coming didn't make it any easier.

I slipped quickly into his thoughts saw the same vision I had a few hours before, but through his eyes.

The pounding of his heart could be felt in my chest as he ran down a street. The pain exploded when he arrived in time to see Mom covered with a white cloth.

A soft cry escaped my lips.

"What are you doing up so late?" Dad grumbled and snatched a cloth to cover the canvas.

"It's morning." I tried to rub the bumps off. After three months of goosebumps, I'd rubbed the soft peach fuzz off my arms. I hoped it wouldn't grow back thick as a gorilla. "Christmas morning. Let's go downstairs."

His mouth formed a slim line and he nodded. "In a minute. I have to wash up."

Pulled by curiosity I asked, "Can I see?"

He shook his head violently. "I just need some peace."

Merry Christmas to you, too.

"Great, sarcasm on Christmas morning. I said I'll be down in a minute. Go on."

On my way downstairs, I heard a soft knock, but there was no one on the porch when I opened the front door. I looked each way and couldn't see anyone on the street, and then I spotted a small white package on the welcome mat. I untied the red ribbon and read the note: "Julie. Thought you might like an Eddie original. No big deal if you don't. Just trash it. Merry Christmas, Eddie."

"Whoa," I said. *Bizarre.* I carefully pulled off the tissue and was stunned to see a pencil drawing of me and Cathy carrying home the Christmas tree. It was really good.

Dad came up behind me.

"That shows some real talent." He peered closely. "Look at the light drawn from your eyes. It's like there's a glow about you, even in pencil. Very nicely done. Who drew it?"

"Eddie. You know, you met him at the market. He left it here."

"You mean that stoner? Why would he give you this?"

"I don't know. It was on the porch."

"Great. A stoner has the hots for my daughter. Thank God we won't be here much longer."

Instead of punching him right in the gut, I ran back upstairs and pinned the drawing on my bulletin board and took a moment to calm down.

Back in the kitchen Dad was moody and I was thinking about Eddie. *Does he really "like me" like me?*

"What the heck happened to you two this morning?" Gramma asked. "I'm ready to celebrate Christmas and you two look like Scrooges."

"I'm sorry, Aurora." Dad's smile was tight. "I got to working last night and I didn't get to sleep."

"Well, try to look a little bit happy for me this morning, will you? After we open gifts, you can go and take a nap."

The tree, nativity set, and the garlands put me more in the mood for celebrating than I had been in the past seven years when we'd exchange gifts over the breakfast table. I cuddled next to

Gramma on the couch and pigged out on chewy gingerbread cookies she made yesterday. Dad stood in the doorway.

"Come sit down by us," Gramma patted the space next to her. "Jewel Anne can play Santa."

Forced into the living room, but not willing to give in, Dad sat in the chair opposite us, but he looked more like he'd sat on a bed of nails. *Merry Christmas, Scrooge.* He jerked his attention to me and I smiled innocently. I didn't want any more bad feelings this morning. I'd had seven crummy Christmases in a row, I'd finally have a good one if it killed me or him.

Gramma spoiled me with a cell phone, pile-lined boots and new clothes. At the bottom of the stack was a small package from Dad. A gift certificate. Big surprise. Trying to stay positive I tried to think it was at least better than nothing. He's not much of a shopper, but he had managed to pick out a scarf for Gramma that he knew she wanted.

"I didn't know what you'd want, so I thought you might like to pick out your own gift," he said. "Well, now that's over, I think I'll take a nap."

"Wait, there's more." I ran upstairs and returned with three packages. *This is either the very best idea or the ultimate worst.*

"I know this is a little spooky—at least to me, but when I was setting up the tree, I found these." I handed one to each of them. I didn't have to say who they were from. They recognized Mom's handwriting.

Gramma caressed her package like it was a kitten. Dad held his out with his fingertips like it was a bomb. "I've been dying to open mine, but I thought I should wait until today. Do you want to go first Dad?"

"No." He shook his head. "This will not bring her back."

"I know." *Duh!* "But just think. Mom picked these out for us. I want to see what she wanted me to have."

"I'll go first." Gramma rubbed the ribbon between her fingers, before pulling it off. She carefully peeled back the tape at each end, without tearing the paper and opened the wrapping to reveal a small box. Inside, nestled in tissue, lay a simple silver bracelet.

"There's an inscription." Gramma's voice choked. She pulled on the reading glasses that hung on a beaded chain around her neck. "To my Mother: I will love you forever. Marina." She slipped the bracelet onto her wrist, then grabbed for a tissue to wipe away her tears. "This is never coming off."

Now more nervous, my hands shook and the goosebumps prickled as I slid the gift open. I unrolled thick tissue paper and a small odd-shaped crystal fell out onto my lap.

"It's another crystal! A mushroom."

"I always thought this one was odd looking." Gramma turned it around in her hands. "She must have wanted you to have it for some reason. It's your turn, Drew. Let's see what Marina wanted you to have."

Dad touched the wrapping then shook his head. "I don't want to open this." He tucked it under his arm and walked to the stairs. "Maybe some things are better left unknown."

We sat there after he left and each stared at our gifts.

"Are you all right, Gramma?" I asked when we were alone.

"Are you?" She pulled me into a deep hug. "I admit, this was a lot more difficult for me than I would have thought. I can understand how your father feels. These gifts—it's like she knew these would be the last gifts she would give us."

Maybe she did?

Curiosity drew me upstairs to the other crystals. Rays of sunlight came through the window, so I set them together and curled up on my bed. Light shown through each piece and the familiar crystal rainbow began on the ceiling. The mushroom did nothing.

But the vision began to appear on the ceiling and I was pulled in.

Another Christmas morning. It was a few days after my mom's funeral. I was lying in front of a tree on my stomach, crying. The scrapes on my knees and arms had hardened into scabs. Gramma came up beside me and began rubbing my back.

"I know it's real hard today. You miss your mom. I do, too. Do you want to open some presents?" I shook my head no. The act cleared the vision and returned me to my room, feeling sad and missing Mom.

"What use was this crystal?" I picked up the mushroom. There was still no control over what I would see. Christmas morning was supposed to be happy. No way would I have picked either of these visions to look at today. *I miss Mom enough already.*

I buried the mushroom and the dolphin in my nightstand and admired Eddie's drawing on the bulletin board.

"Now *that* day was a fun memory. Maybe I should call Eddie." But I chickened out. *He might think I like him.* He was no Jason, but there was something about him that made me feel like he could really understand me.

I started programming my first cell phone. It didn't take long. I only knew three numbers—Dad, Gramma, and Cathy. Tomorrow was New Orleans and I couldn't wait to see if I remembered anything.

Chapter 19

Fine mist turned into steady rain as Gramma pulled off the main highway and onto a dirt road half an hour outside of New Orleans. Although it was just past ten in the morning, thick trees arched over the dark roadway and blocked the winter sun. We reached a fork and Gramma stopped.

"You do know where you're going, right?" I asked.

"Of course," Gramma said. "I haven't been out here in twenty or so years, but I'm pretty sure it's this way." She turned the steering wheel to the right.

"Are you sure or just pretty sure?" I asked. Suddenly, the car dipped and my seatbelt caught as we lurched to a stop.

"Whoa," Gramma said. "That was a deep rut."

"Maybe this is a sign that we should go back," I said. *If we can.*

"It's too late now. The last turn around was a mile back. Besides, we're almost at Miss Beulah's drive."

Gramma used the gear shift to rock the car back and forth until we were finally back on solid ground. Minutes later, the road narrowed again and we crept slowly through a tree-lined tunnel. Silvery-green moss hung from the overhead limbs dipping low enough to skim across the windshield and the wipers were working at full speed. "This is the driveway," Gramma said.

Some driveway. "Maybe this wasn't such a good idea."

Just as the trees seemed to be the thickest, the car nosed into a clearing where a small unpainted house teetered on high stilts near the edge of the muddy bayou.

"That's not her house is it?"

"That's it," Gramma said as she stopped the car. She sounded relieved.

I wasn't. When I opened the door I heard a low sound like a whistle or maybe more like a moan. "This place gives me the creeps." I rubbed at the goosebumps that covered my knees. "I think I'll stay in the car."

"We came all the way out here for you, Jewel Anne. You need to meet the woman who made your crystals." Gramma paused and looked up at the worn house, "Besides, it's not like I'm sending you in there alone."

Mud sucked at my shoes on the short walk across the overgrown yard. The crooked steps leading to the house groaned beneath our weight and when we pushed our way through the sagging screen door, the screech of rusty hinges sent a chill up my spine. The porch was cluttered with old stuffed chairs, a rickety table, and piles of fishing gear.

"Miss Beulah," Gramma called. "Are you home? It's me, Aurora."

There was no answer.

"She must not be here," I said. "Why don't we just leave her a note and go back to your house? Maybe she could come see us in New Orleans."

"She's around here somewhere." I followed Gramma as she made her way back down to the yard and reopened the umbrella. Sharing the small cover, we walked along a gravel trail that wound around the house. On the edge of the slow-moving water an old metal boat rocked. The soft rain was leaving ripples through the water—except for one spot.

"Is that a log?" I backed away. "Or a crocodile?"

"It can't be," Gramma said. She squinted out at the water. "There are no crocodiles in Louisiana—just alligators."

"Oh, good. I feel so much better."

"Come on. There's a shed around here somewhere where Beulah does her glasswork."

I clung to Gramma's arm, my eyes still fixed on the shape in the water. Then, it began to move, creeping toward the shore. "Alligator!" I froze, not sure which way to run.

"Calm down," Gramma said. But her hand shook in mine. The alligator's first step onto land launched us both into motion. We ran down the trail with me pulling on Gramma's hand, urging her to go faster. Relief washed over me when I spotted a building. A shack really. But smoke billowed from a skinny stovepipe at the roofline and light glowed from a narrow window next to the door.

A giant black dog sprang up from the doorway and barked through sharp teeth.

Oh crap! Trapped between the snarling furry mouth in front of me and the long scaly snout at the water's edge, I leaped onto the porch to take my chances with the dog.   Gramma came up behind me and called, "Miss Beulah, oh Miss Beulah. Are you in there? It's me, Aurora." Her voice was calm, as she tried not to disturb either animal.

"Help!" I screamed.

A small woman opened the door and called for the dog to be quiet. Then, without looking at Gramma, she turned to me. "I've been waiting for you, Jewel Anne. Come close and let me get a good look."

I pointed down the steps. "Alligator!"

"That's just Boots. He always likes to see what's going on." Dressed in worn denim overalls with her hair covered by a colorful scarf, the woman's face held so many wrinkles I found myself peering to distinguish features. Her black eyes made direct contact and I had another goosebump attack. The last one hadn't smoothed away yet, so it was a three-story explosion of bumps. "You've certainly taken your time coming to visit me, Aurora," Beulah scolded and wiped her hands on a handkerchief hanging out of her overall pocket. "If you'd waited any longer, I'd have been dead."

"I don't believe that for one minute." Gramma inched around the dog and gave Beulah a hug.

"Come on in to my workshop. I'm sure you'll find it interesting." Beulah opened the door and waved us through.

The room, which smelled of mildew, was long and narrow and lined with shelves filled with glass jars. Some were empty, others held what looked like colored sand. A scarred table sat in the center and a large round iron fireplace blazed in the back. The room was so hot that the windows were fogged over and sweat dropped off the woodwork.

"This is where I created the crystals."

"Crystals for my mother?" I asked.

"Among others."

"How do you make magic crystals?"

"Magic! Aurora, have you taught this girl nothing?" Beulah scoffed. "This isn't magic. The five crystals I made for your mother are no different than any other crystals I've made for hundreds of tourists. The visions are always there. Just not everyone can see."

"Five?" Gramma and I said at the same time.

"We only have four," I said. "This one…" I pulled the winged crystal drop out from under my shirt. "And a brass dolphin jumping over a crystal wave. Then there's a crescent moon and a mushroom."

"There was no mushroom, silly one," Beulah chuckled, the wrinkles on her neck wiggling up and down like a cartoon turkey. "Let's go up to the house. These old bones could use some tea."

Chapter 20

I searched for the alligator before stepping outside and spotted him back in the murky water. I kept my gaze fixed on his dark snout as we climbed back up to the house on stilts. I had expected to see dead chickens inside and bunches of dried herbs hanging from the ceiling.

"Ah!" I screamed and jumped back to the porch. Another seven-foot reptile was sprawled across the living room floor.

Beulah's chuckle was deep and scratchy. "Gets 'em every time. That's Old Boots, Boots' father. He died years ago. He'd always been such good company; I couldn't bear to let him go."

I edged my way around Old Boots and looked for a safe place to stand. On my left there was another stuffed creature—an ugly pig with huge teeth. And on my right, a terrarium held a large snake, lying under a strong light.

"That one's alive," Beulah said. "He's usually out taking care of the mice, but he's got a cold, so I put him in here until he's better. I've always had a way with animals. One of my gifts."

I guess I can be grateful I'm not Mr. Doolittle.

Beulah made the tea from a handful of herbs taken out of a rusty tin can and a dark liquid that looked like bayou water. I had no choice but to drink. The flavor surprised me. It was incredibly sweet and tasted of honey and vanilla and a hint of something like peppermint. I relaxed a little and gazed around the crowded room. Dozens of small crystals hung in the grimy window over a sink filled with dirty dishes. On the stove, a large pot boiled. I could only imagine what was in it. Probably assorted reptile parts and chicken feathers.

"Something smells great," Gramma said.

"That's chicken." Beulah looked directly at me. "I'm boiling it down for soup."

Cathy was always saying she didn't have any privacy. She had no idea.

I sat back in the chair, embarrassed that Beulah seemed to be able to read my mind and stared at the line of crystals. A small breeze from the open window caused them to move and small confetti-sized spots of color began to dance before my eyes, pulling me in.

"Hold on, Jewel Anne," Beulah stepped between me and the crystals. "It's time for me to see what you've brought."

I shook my head to clear my thoughts and try to keep the old woman out of my mind. I emptied my backpack onto the table. Then I took off the winged crystal necklace and set it beside the others.

Beulah touched the necklace, the dolphin, and the crescent moon. "These three help you see into the past events that most influenced your own life—like highlights of your most life-defining moments." She picked up the fourth crystal and laughter crackled out of her. "This is no mushroom," she said. "This is a doorknob."

"Doorknob?" I took the glass ball into my hands and rolled it around. "I guess that's why it didn't do anything. I wonder why my mom wanted me to have it."

"This is the fourth crystal," Beulah said. "It's in the shape of a doorknob because I've always liked crystal doorknobs."

"But it didn't do anything. The other three shine into this rainbow-swirl thing that becomes a vision. This one just sits there."

"Of course." Beulah sighed.

"And so why would I want this?" I coaxed.

"To control your visions. It will allow you to select the past event you need to see in order to make a change."

"How does it work?"

"Like a doorknob."

"And…"

Beulah shook her head. "Hold the knob in your hand and think of where you want to go. Then turn it."

Duh—I might have figured that out if I'd known it was a doorknob! "What about the fifth?" I asked.

"I have to admit, Jewel Anne, that the fifth was always my favorite. The design came to me in the night. The shape was built like flames of a campfire. The fifth can be used only by one whose power is extremely strong. The fifth will allow you to glimpse the future."

"My daughter could see into the future?" Gramma asked. "Why didn't I know this? Why didn't she tell me?"

My bottom lip began to quiver and the tears inside me tried to push their way out. "I can imagine what she must have seen. She must have seen her own ... her own death."

"But why wouldn't she have changed it?" Gramma's voice shook and I grabbed her hand. "Why couldn't she have stayed home that day?"

"I don't know." Beulah turned to face me, her eyes daring me to look away. "On the other hand, you may discover the truth."

I stood to walk around the room, hoping to shake off the layer of creepy I was wearing. "But we still only have four crystals. I don't know what happened to the other one. It could be lost forever."

Beulah caressed the crystals on the table reverently with her calloused hands. "I've made hundreds of crystals, but I would recognize these anywhere," she said. "So Jewel Anne. Tell me about your visions."

Starting at the beginning I poured out my story. Beulah didn't even blink. She just stared as if she didn't hear me. She'd made the crystals, but she clearly didn't get what it was like to work them. "You don't know what I'm going through."

"Let me guess," Beulah said. "You've lost your mother, your father is lost without her, and you are lost somewhere in between. Am I close?"

Okay... She got it. But why does everyone think they know me?

"Which brings me to your gift." Beulah moved across the kitchen and dug into a deep drawer, tossing several odd metal objects onto the counter. I leaned closer to watch. Beulah made mom beautiful crystals with special powers. I couldn't wait to see what I was going to get.

"Here it is." She handed me a small tin box with an advertisement for breath mints.

"Uh, thanks. I'll try to lay off the garlic bread."

"Open it," Beulah said.

I pried open the lid and pulled out a silver bracelet with three little round silver circles hanging from tiny links. Each one read: "Back Space."

"I thought it would be a crystal."

"You have plenty of crystals, besides I'm into recycling now. These are typewriter keys."

"Thanks." I'd never actually seen a typewriter. *Why would you want to make jewelry out of trash?*

"Without your mom or Gramma around, you're going to make mistakes. Each one of these will allow you to back space an event and start again. A "do over." Just pull it off. Remember only one will work each year, so be careful what you use them for."

"I can go back in time?" I wanted to pull one off right now and get back to life before this crap started.

"Only back far enough where you can correct the problem. Then you'll move forward to regular time."

"Next thing you'll be handing me an invisibility cloak!"

"Don't be ridiculous. There's no such thing."

Right now I believe almost anything is possible.

Beulah fastened the bracelet on my wrist. For someone who never wore jewelry before, I was starting to be covered in it.

"Well, now you have a job to do. You need to harness the power of these crystals in order to put back to right what's wrong in your life. Control them. Use them to see what it is you're now blind to."

"What do you mean?"

"What people need changed isn't always apparent in the present. Often you'll need to see what has happened in the past to cause them so much pain. Once you understand that, you'll be better able to channel your energy into positive changes for them."

"Oh God, am I going to start channeling through people now?"

Beulah's mouth opened in a gray-toothed smile. "Find the other crystal and you'll understand."

Chapter 21

We stayed up most of the night talking about everything except Mom. I couldn't get my mind off the death vision. Gramma didn't smile once all night, so I'm guessing she was thinking of Mom too.

Late the next morning Gramma switched on an ancient radio larger than my TV at home. I wasn't surprised when the only station she could tune in played old New Orleans jazz. Everything around me was either old, really old or so old I can't believe how old it is.

"The crystal just has to be somewhere in here," Gramma said as she pulled the chain on the attic ceiling light. "Too bad Rose is gone. She's better at finding things than I am. I've looked through every room, but I waited for you to wake up to tackle this room. Actually, I don't like spiders and wanted the protection."

"From me? Funny, Gramma. How much time do we have?"

"We'll need to leave for the airport by seven."

Keeping a lookout for tiny black creatures, I used a baton with red plastic tassels to brush aside enough cobwebs to open boxes.

The floor was sprinkled with white labels that had once identified the contents of each box. Since the glue was no match for attic heat, we had to open each container. Most held stacks of yellowed receipts, but we did find a few treasures that had belonged to Mom. We set aside a special pile of her things—a ceramic handprint from kindergarten, a christening gown, and a patch-covered Brownie vest.

"It's just not here," Gramma said, a cloud of dust billowing around her as she sat on a chair that looked like the fur on a horses back. "We'll have to hope it's in one of those boxes in Sonoma you haven't unpacked. I can't imagine what else could have happened to it."

I carried the treasures back to Mom's room and crawled back onto the bed I'd left unmade. Brown toile wallpaper like I'd seen on TV covered the slanted ceiling and surrounded me in her memories. The pattern followed an elegantly dressed couple who danced, walked down a flowery lane and sat by a well. They played in a circle around the room as the old yellowed-pattern repeated. Late afternoon sunlight poured into the room. My stomach growled at the same time I picked up the mushroom.

"Should I give you a try?" I unwrapped the crystals and set them on the sill, then took the doorknob into my hand and turned. "Where is the fifth crystal?" I asked.

Rainbow colored light flowed from each of the four crystals to the ceiling where a vision began to form. It was Mom about my age. She stood in this very room and held a wooden box. Then she knelt down. Her hand touched the familiar toile wallpaper and a panel opened up. She placed the box inside the wall and left.

The vision cleared and I tried to breath deeply to calm down. It didn't work. Too freaky. Focusing on the walls again, I followed the toile couple dancing and walking and sitting at the well. Goosebumps grew in their own pattern up my arms. The toile pattern repeated itself around the room. Dancing, walking, well, dancing, walking, well, then dancing, walking, dancing, *oops!*

Kneeling down in the corner, next to the bathroom doorway, I touched the dancing pair with my fingertips, then ran my hand over the toile. The wall felt like any other—hard. But when I pressed, a small door sprang open.

"Gramma!" I jumped back. "Gramma, come here!"

Gramma ran into the room, her breath ragged. "What is it, Jewel? Are you all right?"

"Look at this! I used the doorknob like Beulah said and asked what happened to the fifth crystal. I saw Mom put a box in here!"

"Well, my goodness. There are several hiding places for valuables in this old house, but I don't remember this one." Gramma knelt down and peered inside. "I can't see anything. It's too dark."

"I know Mom hid the crystal here."

"Let me get a flashlight and we can check it out. Unless you'd like to just reach your hand in there now."

"Yeah, right."

The beam from the flashlight lit up the cubbyhole. Inside was the wooden box I had seen in the vision. I used a washcloth from the bathroom to pull it out into the room. "This must have been in here a long time," I said. "The crystal is in here. I can feel it."

"We're lucky it's hidden up here," Gramma said. "It never would have made it through the last hurricane. I had to gut the whole first floor. Let's get it open."

It took longer to find a flathead screwdriver than it did to pry open the lid. "I got it!" I cried as it flung open. We stared silently into the box for a moment. A small leather-bound book read, "Marina's Diary."

"We gave it to her for her sixteenth birthday." Gramma's eyes teared. "Along with the necklace you're wearing. I'd completely forgotten about it. And look. There's a picture of your mom and dad at the beach. They must have only been sixteen."

The picture showed the young pair sitting on a log with what must have been the Gulf of Mexico in the background. Mom was smiling and looked so happy. Dad was hamming it up for the camera, flexing his muscles as he posed with his surfboard.

"We thought we were going on a family vacation to Florida, just the three of us," Gramma said. "I should have known they couldn't be separated for two whole weeks. He followed us in his car for hours until he ran out of gas. We saw him pull off the road and had to take him along. That boy."

"Ew, what's that?" I poked at some blond fuzz in the box.

"That would be a lock of your dad's hair."

"Gross. Why would she want that?"

"Young love, my dear. Young love."

"But there's no crystal," I sighed. "I guess the doorknob was wrong. Or maybe it was moved."

I opened the brown cover and read the first entry. "My 16th birthday started out so well and got really bizarre. Two things: my period started and I think my mom may be losing her mind. You won't believe what she said to me today!"

Between the goosebumps and my nerves my hands were shaking so hard that I had to close the book. "Do you think I should read this?"

"I think you need to. But, as her mother, I'm sure she never intended for me to see it." Gramma stood up and brushed the tears off her cheeks.

"Well, we need to hurry now or we'll be late for our flight. Do you have room in your backpack or shall I pack the box?"

"I'll make room."

As we pulled away in the cab, I looked back at the soft pink house, rainwater still dripping from the iron balcony. *I could live here.*

We checked our bags and waited in the long security line. Gramma took off her jewelry, shoes, and jacket to avoid the buzz of the security gate. I placed my backpack on the conveyer belt, walked easily through the metal detector, and waited at the other side for Gramma to pull herself back together and for my backpack to come out.

The guard stopped the belt when my backpack appeared on his screen. He stared at it for several long moments and then moved it forward and began to search through the contents. Finally, he pulled the wooden box out and placed it back on the belt for another trip through the machine. "What's in there?" he asked.

"An old diary and some personal items," Gramma said, coming up behind me.

He stopped the belt and stared closely at the monitor. "Could you open this please?" I took the box from him and worked the latch open. The guard removed the diary and photo, leaving the fuzzy hair at the bottom. Then, he placed it back on the belt.

"What's the problem? We just found this box today. It belonged to my late daughter."

By now the line was growing quite long behind them. The guard moved us to a side table where we stood while he continued to study the box. After the third screening, he gave it back. We repacked everything and checked in. While we waited for our flight home we studied the thick dark wood.

Once we boarded the plane and settled in, I opened the diary. Mom's handwriting was sloppy, but I read until my eyes stung.

"Dear Diary,

Mom is freaked out! I keep getting goosebumps even though it's hot and muggy outside and she says it's because I have some "special powers!" Yeah right! She's nuts! Except for that, my birthday was pretty good. I got the new jacket I wanted. I can't wait until it's cold enough to wear it.

Love Marina."

Several weeks of entries showed me that mom's life had been eerily similar to mine. There was the same denial that slowly became acceptance. I closed my eyes for a minute to rest them and was awakened by a flight attendant asking me to move my seat back up. We were ready to land. I stretched as much as I could in the confined space. I hurt all over. *Red-eye flight? They should call this the red-butt flight.*

"It was like you said, Gramma. It's been the same for me as it was for Mom."

"Did she write anything about me?"

"Only that she thought you must be losing your mind."

"That's not surprising," Gramma patted my hand. "How did you like New Orleans?"

"It was great," I wondered how to put my next words. "Actually Gramma, I'd really like to live with you. That is, if I can't talk Dad into staying in Sonoma."

"What brought this on?"

"I'm tired of being alone. I just don't want to move anymore."

"I understand sweetheart and I'd love to have you. But I think you and your dad belong together. You'll work things out. You've got the power now. Besides I'm always at work. You'd be alone too much."

I'm alone all the time now.

Chapter 22

On the afternoon of New Year's Eve, I woke up in my own bed, happy to be surrounded by my things. I pulled on thick socks and padded down to the kitchen where Dad sat at the table.

"I'm glad you're up." Dad refilled his coffee mug. "Cathy's been over here twice looking for you and I don't think I could put her off any longer."

He was in pain. I knew it, but all I could say was, "You look tired."

"I couldn't sleep last night." His dark sunken eyes and the slump of his shoulder looked like he hadn't slept in a week.

Cathy hammered on the door before letting herself in.

"You're so lucky." Cathy pulled me up to my room. "Imagine getting to fly off to New Orleans. That must have been so cool. What did you do? Did you see any alligators? Did you ride in one of those horse-drawn carriages? Did you eat gumbo? What is gumbo? Tell me about every minute." Cathy immediately spotted Eddie's drawing. "Oh my God, where did you get this? It's so cute. Wait, Eddie made this? It looks just like us. I didn't know he could draw so well."

"Neither did I. He left it on my porch Christmas morning. He said if I didn't want it, I should throw it away."

"Oh, no, you don't. If you don't want this, I do. I don't remember seeing him after we picked out the tree. He must have been watching us. Creepy, eh?"

"Yeah, I thought of that too. But it's such a great picture I wanted to keep it anyway. Besides, he seems pretty harmless once you get to know him a little."

"If you say so. But I have this feeling there's some bad news waiting to catch up with him. I wouldn't want to be anywhere near when it does."

"I don't know, but I do think I understand him better now that I know about his mother."

"You mean the hermit lady?"

"Don't call her that. She's really sick."

"Really? Now I feel terrible. Have you heard something I haven't?"

"Eddie takes care of her. I've seen him at the market quite a few times picking up food and prescriptions for her. One day I happened to be in their neighborhood," I skipped over the part about me stalking him, "and I saw her on the front porch. She had a scarf around her head and it looked like she had no hair, like she was on chemo or something."

"Bummer. He's a weird guy, but now I feel sorry for him. And he's helping her? Wow. Hard to picture. Well, it may explain the marijuana. Could be his mom's medical supply."

I hadn't thought of that.

"I hate knowing this," Cathy said. "Now I feel like I have to start being nicer to him. And I really like the picture. Let's take it to the copy store and make one for me. Hey, new bracelet?" Cathy turned the silver chain around to read the inscription. "What are these things?"

"Beul...an old lady Gramma knows gave it to me. They're typewriter keys."

"Well, it's different," Cathy said.

"I kind of like it now. It's grown on me." It was my safety net. I just wish I knew what was going to happen to me when I pulled one off.

Ice still lay thick on the windshields when I walked Cathy home the next morning. The sky was a clear blue and the air crisp. No one seemed to be out and about. Cathy had to clean house all day on the first—a family tradition.

"A clean house on the first day of the year will remain clean all year long," Dolores said.

"Yeah, because we clean it all year long," Cathy complained.

"Now you run along, Julie," Dolores said. "You don't have to help."

Leaving was okay with me. The diary was calling me. I bundled back into my jacket and left the warmth of Cathy's house.

So much had happened these past months—still seemed to be happening—that I liked the walk alone in the cold. The hills surrounding me held rows of leafless grape vines shooting out in all directions.

Back in my room, I sat cross-legged on the bed and drew a deep breath before reading Mom's words:

"Dear Diary, Mom took me out to thank Beulah for making the crystal necklace. She's nice, but must be about one hundred years old! Her place is creepy in a neat way. She wouldn't let go of my hand and the goosebumps were crawling over me like ants. Finally she smiled and let go and said I'd need to see all the crystals. She made Mom stay back to stir a pot of something boiling on the stove and took me out to her workshop. In one hand she placed a small crescent moon and in the other a dolphin splashing in water. So cute. Until they started to glow red in my hands! Then colors like a rainbow appeared on the ceiling and showed a picture of Mom in the kitchen still stirring the soup!

I asked how she did it and she said it was me. It got even stranger when she brought out the next crystal. A doorknob. How weird is that? She showed me how to use it to tune in the visions to what I wanted. Like I wanted any vision!! The last crystal looked like a campfire. I thought it was ugly, but I didn't tell her. She said they would be useful when I needed to know about the future to help someone.

But she asked me not to use the fifth crystal until I'd told Mom all about them. I don't plan to say anything ever. I'll just use them to decorate my room.

Love, M."

Eager to know what Mom had gone through with the crystals I turned the dated page, but there was scribbling I couldn't read. Then the dates jumped weeks ahead.

"Dear Diary, I'm sorry it's been so long since my last entry. I can't even begin to tell you how horrible it's been. I can't even tell Mom. The crystals gave me a vision! It was me, only much older. I was walking with a little girl. She looked like me, so I think she was my daughter. We were crossing the street and she ran out ahead of me and a car hit her! She flew like a Raggedy Ann doll and when she landed, I knew she was dead. It was so creepy that I threw the crystal campfire at the wall, but it didn't break! I hate it! I'm going to hide it away, so it can never be found. I've decided I can never be married and never have children. I'll have to go through my life as alone as I am now. At least I have you.

Love, M."

"Uh!" I gasped so hard, I think I swallowed a bug. I reread the entry. Mom had seen the accident coming. But I was supposed to die, not her. I turned my head so my tears wouldn't run the ink. No wonder she didn't tell Gramma about the crystals. Mom knew that one of us was going to die.

My shaking hand turned the page. The vision was not mentioned during the next several weeks of diary entries, but there was a heaviness to everything. Mom worked to help change the life of a friend from school. And she helped an elderly neighbor, and a kid with no friends. But during the summer, she met a boy—Drew—and the tone of the last pages of the diary changed completely.

"Dear Diary, Drew is so cute and so cool. I love him so much. I know we're going to get married. I'm supposed to be a Changer, well, now I'll change my future. When we have a little girl, I'll watch her like a hawk and never let her cross any street without holding my hand. There's a lot I'm not sure of, but I KNOW I'll keep her safe. But the fifth crystal is like a Magic 8 Ball. Every time I shake things up, I get a different answer. Mom's taking me to Sonoma. I can't wait. Ever since I read The Valley of the Moon, that's been part of the picture when I think of happily ever after. Maybe the future can be whatever I want it to be. If I can't, I'll make that ugly crystal fix things for them.

Love, M."

I tried to swallow past the lump in my throat. Mom was so strong. She believed her love could save her child—me. And it did. But how was the crystal going to fix anything for me and Dad? The remaining blank pages left no clue.

Chapter 23

Closing the diary I rested it back into the box and hid it in my closet. *I miss you, Mom.* I went to the guest room and sat on the bed, pressing the pillow to my face. It still smelled like Gramma. I couldn't remember what Mom smelled like. My pathetic life just reached a new low.

Cathy had a family. I envied her cleaning all day. I decided to copy her family traditions since I the only tradition I had was whining.

Wandering into the living room I dropped onto the couch. The branches of the Christmas tree sagged under the weight of the ornaments and the needles were falling to the floor. What had seemed like such a warm room now looked sad. "I have to do something."

Taking it down was definitely not as much fun as putting it up. It took two hours to box everything up, drag the boxes up to the attic closet, and drag the tree to the sidewalk where the Girl Scouts Tree Removal service would pick it up. After I vacuumed up the stray needles and dusted the mantle, the empty room still felt nothing like Cathy's warm and friendly living room. I had to do something. I scavenged through the house for family photos.

Except for last year's not too hideous school picture, they were pretty old. But I managed to find one of Mom and Dad together and one of my grandparents for the mantle.

The Christmas bouquet Gramma bought was dead, but the vase cleaned up nicely and I filled it with several long twigs of berry-covered holly from the yard.

The room was still missing something, but looked warmer—like a family actually lived here. Above the couch was a large empty wall with the one nail where Cathy and I had hung a wreath. Dad should have a picture I could hang here.

Goosebumps appeared on my arm at the landing and I almost turned around, but something pulled me up. The open studio door gave me a view of him sitting with his head in his arms. His shoulders were shaking and I knew he was crying. *Turn and run!* But my feet moved me inside. He didn't hear me come up beside him and was as surprised as I was when I placed my hand on his shoulder.

"Julie?" Dad looked up and wiped his face quickly. "You should have knocked."

"I'm sorry, your door was open and I saw you sitting here," I stammered and stepped back. "I thought you might need something." His gift from Mom was still wrapped on his desk.

He lifted the gift and placed it on a high shelf. I really wanted to know what was in that box. It was like another piece of Mom's life that I could know her by.

"Enough of this. I have work to get back to." He pulled up his chair. "What did you want?"

"Oh, I took down the tree and put everything away. The room looks so empty I wanted to put something up," I babbled. "There's a big blank wall behind the couch. I thought you might have something you've done that we can hang there."

"I doubt I have anything suitable, but help yourself to that crate over there. There's some old stuff I know I won't sell."

I rummaged through the open crate. A large framed painting of a hillside covered in vineyards caught my eye. "This looks like Sonoma. Can I hang this one up?"

He looked at the painting and the pain on his face caused a shiver up my spine. "I forgot about that. Your mom and I traveled to France on our honeymoon. I painted it from a picture she took for our first anniversary. It used to hang in our living room in New Orleans."

He actually mentioned Mom? "If you don't want me to, I won't hang it."

"It doesn't matter," Dad said gruffly. "Do what you want."

You don't have to growl.

"What?"

"Nothing." I carried it downstairs and hung it above the couch. I stared at it for a while until I thought maybe it looked familiar. What other memories does he have crated up?

After a dinner Gramma had left for us, I sat in the living room and admired my work. Dad paused in the doorway.

"What do you think of it?" I asked. "I worked all day in here. It's not perfect, but doesn't it seem more like a home now?"

"I have a project to get back to," Dad said. He left without even stepping over the threshold.

"I'm so tired of his moods," I said. "I don't care if he likes it or not. I'm sick of living out of a U-haul. Even if he pulls me away in June, it will be kicking and screaming from a house that looks and feels like a home!"

Chapter 24

The cold aluminum bench made me wish I had some junk in my trunk or was wearing five layers of jeans on the first day back to school. Back to the drama that is my life.

I ignored Cathy's chatter and watched Eddie walk across the quad toward the lunch tables. He caught my eye so I smiled a little, then looked away. He had given me a nice gift but I didn't want people to again start thinking we were a couple.

"Hey, Eddie," Cathy grabbed his arm as he passed our lunch table. "Sit down."

What? Now she had my attention.

"I loved the picture you drew of us," Cathy said to Eddie. "I hope you don't mind, but we made a copy over break so I could have one in my room too."

"Okay." Eddie raised his shoulders in surprise. He walked around the table and sat in front of me.

"How long have you been drawing?" Cathy added.

"A while. Mr. Rush gave me the sketchbook and got me started." He answered Cathy, but he kept his eyes on me and grinned.

Oh, great. He likes me.

"Why don't you play ball any more?" Cathy asked. "Thomas said you were really good."

Anger erased the smile off his face. "I don't have the time. I'm busy after school."

"Really?" Cathy said, even as I elbowed her in the ribs. "What with?"

"Just stuff."

I asked a question of my own: *How's it going at home Eddie?*

Eddie's thoughts exploded in my head. *If my damn dad hadn't left, I'd still have a life.*

I hated it when Eddie could read my thoughts. Now that I could read his, it wasn't much better. At least I know his relationship with his dad sucks.

"I have to go," he said, then nodded at me. "See ya."

"That was weird," I said to Cathy after he left. "What made you call him over?"

"At first I just thought he was weird. But now I think he might need a few new friends," Cathy said. "Friends that don't look for the next opportunity to commit a crime. I have a way of knowing these things."

Why didn't I think of that?

The bell rang and I walked to science but stood outside and took a deep breath. A large cloud of warm air formed as I exhaled. It was as if a cartoon bubble appeared that read "I'm afraid to see

Kelly again." *Get over it—go in!* Miss Day was unrolling a screen hanging in front of the classroom to reveal a list of names as I plopped into a seat.

"Here are your new lab partners for this semester. Move to your lab seats and we'll start at chapter twenty two."

I scanned for my name. Next to it read "Jason." *Jason is my lab partner? No way!* Peeking around my book I tried to see his reaction, but he was turned away. Kelly wasn't. She stared right at me and glared. Then she walked to Miss Day. I didn't hear Kelly's question or the teacher's answer, but I could tell from Kelly's frown she didn't like what she'd heard.

Miss Day spoke to the class. "There will be no changes. You've been teamed so the stronger student can work with the one who needs help."

So much for keeping my bad grades private.

Picking up my backpack I walked to my lab station and pulled out my notebook. I tried to look busy as I slowly wrote my name in the top right hand corner. I did have nice handwriting. It was my own combination of printing and cursive. I particularly like my J's. *My life may suck, but I've got the autograph of a rock star.*

The lab stool next to me scraped against the tile floor, but I kept my eyes on the page.

"Hey," Jason said.

"Uh…hey," I said. Okay, I really squeaked, but at least sound came out. I thought of tons to say like 'seeing you smile really brightens up my life and if you don't have any other plans maybe we could go to the movies or get married and raise beautiful children with gorgeous teeth like yours.' *And that smile? He is so cute.*

Kelly walked to the table behind us and glared at me as she passed.

"What's up with her?" Jason asked. "She really gave you the stink eye."

"Gave me what?"

"The stink eye. A dirty look. What'd you do?"

I shrugged. What could I say? For a great looking guy, Jason had no clue about three things. One: Kelly hated my guts. Two: Kelly loved Jason. Three: Kelly hated my guts.

Saturday morning the sun cracked through the rain clouds and I had enough winter sunlight to think about trying the crystals starting with Kelly.

With the dolphin on the sill beneath the crescent moon and the doorknob in my hand, I asked, "Why does Kelly hate her life?"

A bright light flared in front of me. It cleared into a swirling rainbow. A nine or ten-year-old version of Kelly appeared. She jumped out of the passenger side of a car as soon as it pulled into a driveway wearing shorts and a t-shirt with a camp logo.

"Kelly, don't forget your bag," the driver called.

"In a minute, Dad. I want to see Mom." She pushed open the front door and ran through. "Mom! Mom, I'm home!"

"In here." Kelly followed the woman's voice into a large living room lined on one side by floor-to-ceiling glass doors that overlooked a lush valley. Her mother, dressed in a beige suit almost disappeared against the same color of the long beige couch. Kelly jumped on the couch and wrapped her arms around her mother.

"Really, Kelly," her mother said, unpeeling herself. "You need to wash that travel smell off of you. And we have company."

Kelly saw the older woman, sitting in a chair opposite them, for the first time. "I'm sorry," Kelly said.

"I hate to disturb your homecoming," the woman smiled kindly and started to stand. "I can wait outside while you two catch up."

"Nonsense. It's only been a month," Mrs. Alazar said. "Kelly, this is Miss Meecham. She's the director at the Northspur Camp for girls. We're very lucky. She's going to make a space for you at her camp. Please thank her."

"Thank you, Miss Meecham. I'll see you next summer."

"Oh, I'm afraid you don't understand," Miss Meecham said, a sympathetic look on her face. "It's for the rest of this summer."

"But Mom," Kelly pleaded, "I just got home. What about our family vacation?"

"That was before your father was invited to speak at a legal conference in London. Now be a good girl and run upstairs and shower. I've already packed a fresh bag and Miss Meecham will drive you to the camp herself."

"But..." Kelly started.

Her father stood behind her and placed his hand on her shoulder. "Now I know you want to make us proud, right?"

Kelly looked pleadingly at Miss Meecham, who looked sad, too, but shrugged.

"Yes, Dad," Kelly said, then walked slowly upstairs. In her room, she sat on her pink ruffled bed and let tears run down her face. The soft tears turned into a torrent and she fell back on her bed sobbing. As she struggled to catch a breath, her sad face turned angry and she began to pound at the perfectly arranged pile of pillows.

"Freak out!" I tossed the crystal on the bed like it was on fire. I wasn't prepared to feel pity for Kelly. What should I do about it? Did I want to do anything? She wasn't a little girl anymore. She should tell her parents how she feels. Okay, that sounded stupid. I couldn't even do that.

Chapter 25

After a week as Jason's lab partner, I began to speak in full sentences. I still hadn't figured out what to do with Kelly. But priorities, right? Every time I was around her, she would make sure I was looking and then whisper something to someone next to her and they'd all laugh. Tough on the old self-esteem.

Too lazy to shower again before I met Cathy at the movies on Friday night, I stuck my head under the bathtub faucet and washed my hair. Then I touched up the polish on my toes and slid into flip flops. Hopefully, I'd be able to dry my hair and leave without running into Dad. I'd made an art out of avoiding him. . . or maybe he avoided me. Oh, who cared anyway? The battery on my phone was dead, so I plugged it in and left without seeing him.

Cathy and Thomas were in front of the old theatre talking to someone that looked like—*no way!*—Jason! Even his teeth were cute. I moved awkwardly toward them, hoping my hair was okay and that nobody else was wearing the same shirt. I especially hoped no one else needed my help.

"Hey, Julie," Cathy said, her eyebrows raising with a message I didn't get. "You know the guys, right?"

"Yeah. Jason's my lab partner." *Like I hadn't told Cathy about it the second I got out of class.*

"Hey," Jason said. Then he smiled. At me. I nodded my head. I think. Mesmerized by his smile, I had nothing to say. I looked down at my orange flip flops. The matching polish on the big toe of my right foot was smeared.

"I heard this movie was great from two girls at school, but my mom said it got poor reviews and would be a waste of money," Cathy said. "Like going to the movies could ever be a waste, and anyway, this theatre always has the best popcorn, you know. It doesn't taste oily. Come on, let's go in."

Cathy led me to the small candy counter. We lined up in front of Jason and right behind Eddie. Luck was not with me tonight. Kelly stood in front of Eddie and turned at the sound of Jason's voice. She saw me first.

"Hey, Jason, come up here with us," Kelly said.

"That's okay, I'm with Julie."

He's with me? Even with Eddie's and Kelly's shocked faces, I'd have to bet that mine was the most stunned.

"You're gonna get it," Kelly hissed in my ear. Then she smiled at Jason.

I had no idea what "it" was, but I had no doubt it would hurt.

Cathy pulled me back with her and whispered, "Let me smack her in the head."

"Ignore her."

"Just a little smack?" Cathy asked.

Cathy was so easy to like.

Kelly paid for a large soda and took one last jab at me as I passed. "You should take more care who you hang with," she whispered. "Your little girlfriend here is nothing but a loser."

Nobody talked about my friend that way. I wanted to tear the brat's hair out. But at the same time I wanted to climb into a hole and disappear. Angry goosebumps reappeared with a force that chilled my entire body. I shivered and then jumped back as the drink in Kelly's hand splattered on the floor.

"Oh," Kelly moaned to the counter clerk. "These cheap cups. Look at this mess. Give me another soda."

The manager came up behind the clerk. "I saw everything," he said. "You crushed the cup yourself. I won't give you another drink, I'll give you the mop. I'm tired of you teenagers coming in here acting like you own the place."

Thomas, Jason, and Cathy were laughing. Eddie wasn't. He was staring. At me.

Once inside, I followed Cathy and Thomas into a row near the front, which left Jason sitting at my right. Cathy's strange little eyebrow wave meant the seating arrangement had not been an accident. I pushed back far into the red velvet fabric. When I failed to disappear into the seat completely, I inhaled the butter-soaked popcorn at a furious rate and stared at the opening credits like they were messages from God. *Kelly's gonna kill me!*

Cathy's mom had nailed the review—the movie sucked and my mind began to wander. I could feel Kelly's eyes boring into my skull. Glancing over my right shoulder, I saw her staring directly at me, even in the dark. A quick turn to my left revealed that Eddie couldn't take his eyes off me either. *Isn't anyone watching this crappy movie?*

What could I do? It was like I was cheating on my powers. Could making the ones I'm supposed to be changing unhappy be good for me? Those powers probably don't want me sitting here next to Jason. They would want me to make sure Kelly gets him, because maybe that would make her happy. But what about my happiness? My first knee-buckling, stomach flipping kiss?

"Ah!" I screamed and I threw my half-full popcorn bag into the air when something landed on my shoulder. Several people behind me hissed, "Shh!" as I realized the "something" was Jason's arm.

"Sorry," he whispered in my ear. "Just stretching."

Thomas rocked in his chair cracking up.

"I'll be right back," I lied. I planned to spend the rest of my life in the ladies' room. No way could I go back in and sit next to Jason.

I tried not to look at Kelly or Eddie when I passed, but I did anyway. Eddie looked sad, and the eye darts Kelly threw were so sharp that I missed the step in the doorway and stumbled into the lobby. The swinging door hit me on the butt as I straightened in front of the bored-looking snack bar crew. *I'm never going to another movie again in my life.* I tried to keep myself from running to the sanctuary of the restroom. The butter spots grew into larger stains when I added a little water. I squatted in front of the hand dryer until my shirt was dry.

What's with Jason? No boy has ever put his arm around me before. I played with the backspace charm in my bracelet. I would love to pull, but I only get one a year and is this really the worst thing that would happen to me all year? *Uh! I hate perspective!*

What does it mean? Does he *like* me? There were no answers to be found in the bathroom, so I took a deep breath and headed back into the dark theatre.

During the rest of the long dull movie, I pressed against the armrest that separated me from Cathy, keeping guard over the space between me and Jason. He seemed to have the same idea. Together we created a gap large enough for another person. *Lovely, Jules. Ya blew it.* I won't have to worry about Kelly's feelings again. He'll never speak to me again after tonight.

We stood outside waiting for Dolores to take us home. Kelly and Eddie stood apart watching. Maybe they should start going out and get me out of the middle.

"Are you going to the dance tomorrow?" Jason asked me. "I hope we can dance together."

Shock stuck in my throat like a popcorn kernel and I started coughing. Kelly was only ten feet away and from the look on her face, she'd heard every word. Her thoughts screamed at me. *You can't go with her! You're supposed to like me!*

I didn't hear anything from Eddie, but his body language read pissed.

"Uh, I don't know if I'm going…" even though Cathy and I had spent three days picking out just the right dress to wear. "I have to ask my dad."

The instant Dolores' car pulled away from the curb Cathy started in. "Oh my God—he so likes you. Just before you got here Thomas said that Jason said he thought you were cute. I tried to call you, but you didn't pick up. They wanted to sit with us. I nearly peed my pants when he put his arm around you and popcorn flew everywhere."

"You should have warned me he was coming."

"There wasn't time," Cathy said. "But he is so cute and really nice. And I know you like him. And he wants to dance with you!"

"Great! Kelly isn't going to like this," I murmured as we pulled up to my dark house. I don't like the negative attention she brings to me and I am supposed to be helping her. Damnit!

"So what?" Cathy said. "It's about time she didn't get something she wanted."

But I knew there was a lot she wanted and couldn't have. Like caring parents. But it was hard to feel sorry for someone who hated my guts.

"You don't sound very happy," Cathy said. "He seems like a great guy and you think he's cute and all, so I can't figure out why you're not excited. I'd be excited if I were you. I'd be thrilled if Thomas would ask me."

"I just feel funny," I said. "This is my first dance and…"

"Your first dance?" Cathy exclaimed. "Didn't your junior high have dances? We had a dance once a month if we kept the campus clean. It was the only thing during eighth grade I liked. It was so much fun. Don't you like to dance?"

"Uh, I don't know. I've been meaning to tell you that . . . well, I don't really know how."

"Oh—my—God," Cathy said.

"It's real bad, isn't it?" My heart raced and I flashbacked to the CPR class we just finished in PE. *Am I too young for a heart attack?*

She took me by the shoulders, looked me in the eyes and said…nothing. Cathy was speechless.

Now I was really scared.

Chapter 26

Cranking up the music, my feet practiced the dance steps Cathy taught me while my lips practiced kissing in front of the mirror on my door.

He'd actually said he wanted to dance with me. There were witnesses. Too many witnesses, maybe. It's possible—slim, I know—I could fall into his lips during a song and he might not mind or notice as long as I don't fall so hard I knocked out a tooth. I'd get my first kiss.

"Knock!" The mirror rattled and shocked me to a stop. Feeling guilty like there was something to hide, I opened the door.

"Can you turn your music down?" Dad yelled. "I have a headache."

I shut the door and turned it down. A little. *Didn't he remember being young? My first dance. This is a big deal!*

I brushed my wet hair and checked the clock. Two hours until Cathy picked me up. I wish she were here now. Actually, I wish Mom was here! Was she worried about her first dance with Dad? Was he? The crystal necklace grew warm against my skin. Curiosity pulled me to the other crystals. Holding Beulah's doorknob I moved to the window and let myself fall into the developing vision. *Were my parents worried?*

The colors around me changed from yellow and orange, to red. Blood red. The swirl stopped and I saw Mom's face, the blood dripping from a cut on her forehead.

The scene ran backwards. The car hit my mom one moment and then we were back on the sidewalk holding hands the next. Mom stood on the corner of the park and looked at her watch, probably wondering what had kept Dad.

The colors swirled together into a murky brown, then formed into a restaurant. Dad sat laughing at a large round table filled with other men his age. It was strange to see him so happy. Joking around and having a good time. "So it's settled, then," he said. "We'll go to Australia for a week of awesome surfing." He looked at his watch. "Crap! I'm late."

"What's up?" asked the guy next to him.

"I was supposed to pick up Marina and Jewel at the park a half an hour ago. Her car is in the shop."

"Hang out here some more. The park's only four blocks away. They can walk."

"You don't know Marina, she's really weird about walking places with Jewel. Besides, Jewel has a dentist appointment. I better run." On the way to the park, he checked his watch several times. Traffic began to back up several blocks before he reached the park. His body jolted at the first wail of the siren. Traffic stopped completely. No place to turn around. A fire truck, followed closely by an ambulance passed them by.

He threw the gearshift into park and bolted from the car, leaving the door open and the engine running. He ran to a crowd gathered on the sidewalk staring into the street. He pushed his way through and froze as he saw Mom's face the last seconds before she was covered by a white sheet.

"Where's Jewel Anne? Jewel Anne! Please, God, not Julie, too!" He alternated between gasping for breath and forgetting to breathe all together. Then he saw me, sitting in the back of the patrol car, crying. He ran to me and held me tight. One half of his heart was saved. The other half was gone.

The vision cleared and I threw the crystal against the headboard. I'd wanted to know if dances made them nervous, too, not how worried they were in their worst experience of their lives!

I dragged myself down to the kitchen. Dad sat at the table picking through a pile of unmatched socks. *He's the last one I want to see. I'm already depressed enough.*

"Thanks a lot. Great to see you, too."

"I didn't say, I mean, I didn't mean that." I pulled a juice box out of the refrigerator and stuck the straw in the small hole as I absorbed what I'd seen in the vision. *He feels responsible for Mom's death.*

He gasped loudly and my hand clenched, squirting juice all over the floor.

"What do you know about that? Did Aurora say something?"

"No!" My hands shook as I bent to wipe up the mess. *I should run now. Fast.* "No. It's just that . . . it's just that I know you were supposed to be there. But you were late."

Tears dropped out of Dad's eyes and he leaned against the counter like he was melting. "It's true. It was my fault."

"No, it wasn't! It was an accident," my voice faded. Dad had already run out of the room. I should have followed him. He was so upset. *But what could I say?* I hid out in my room and worried about his feelings when I needed to be getting ready for the dance.

I was dressed and ready to go, when I decided I was too depressed to go anywhere. I pulled my pajamas from under my pillow when I heard Cathy climbing the steps. She was wearing a black jacket buttoned up to her neck.

"Your dad hasn't seen the dress yet, has he?" I asked.

"What gave me away?"

"Oh, I don't know. The full trench coat, maybe?" It wasn't that her dress was very low cut, it was just that the boobs Cathy had been waiting for had finally arrived. Perfect Bs. I guess I'd have to start believing in the power of positive thinking.

Chapter 27

Red and white decorations filled the hall and helium-filled balloons floated at the ceiling of the transformed gym, but only a handful of students were standing in small groups along the walls. From what I could tell, they were all freshmen.

Jason and Thomas showed up a few minutes later and we decided to stake out an area near the DJ. Jason had a beautiful grin on his face. "Your dad said yes, huh? Cool."

Cathy kicked her shoes off and ran to put in a song request. It took me longer to unbuckle the strappy sandals. I had one off and one on when Eddie appeared by my side.

I wish she'd dump Jason and go out with me. The shock of Eddie's thought made me lose my balance and I slipped right to the hardwood floor, landing on my knees.

"Whoa," Eddie said, lunging without catching me. "That was random. It looked like a sniper got you." He reached out a hand, but then I felt two hands on my waist, lifting me up.

"You okay?" Jason asked. Although we'd been lab partners for more than a month, it was the first time we'd touched. Well, if you didn't count the popcorn tossing nightmare. I managed to nod. "Then let's dance."

"Okay." I felt Eddie watching us walk to the dance floor, but when I turned, he was gone.

Jason's hand was cool and dry. It wouldn't be for long, though. Mine was hot and sweaty. At least it was a fast dance. *Did Mom feel this weird at her first dance?*

I looked around—at the other kids, at the DJ, at the food table and the pennants on the gym walls . . . . anywhere but making eye contact with Jason. I hoped I was dancing okay. My knees were sore, but no one was staring, so maybe I didn't look like a camel on roller skates. Maybe I looked like I knew what I was doing?

My confidence lasted for precisely two songs. Then the first slow dance began.

Jason put his hands on my hips and I placed my hands on his shoulders. There was an awkward space between us. *Am I supposed to talk?* I'd forgotten to ask Cathy. After a few penguin turns, Jason readjusted his hold and pulled me into a close embrace. With his shoes still on and mine off, he was much taller.

My face smashed into his shoulder. I turned my head out to the side and kept the beat in an effort not to stumble. I'd never been this close to a guy before—or been held like this. I had imagined it would be romantic. But my neck was stiffening and my nose was dangerously close to his underarm after the fast dancing and the heat in the room.

The crystal necklace grew hot on my skin. As we circled to face one side of the room, Kelly watched us. Either it was bad lighting or she looked like she was going to cry. I didn't want to hear her thoughts, but the flood gate was open tonight. I couldn't stop it.

Oh, Jason, so much for having one good thing in my life. That scag.

And then we turned to the other side and I saw Eddie watching—his thoughts tore past Kelly's.

Julie looks so pretty tonight.

Okay, that wasn't too hard to hear. But each time we circled, I heard more and more of the same—*scag, pretty, scag, pretty*—like Eddie and Kelly were each screaming at each other through my ears. I shivered.

Jason gave me a little hug. "I like dancing with you, too," he said. "I told Kelly on the first day of school that I thought you were real cute. But she said you were going out with Eddie."

"Oh," I croaked. *That's another reason why Kelly hates me.*

"Would you like to go out with me?"

"Go out?" He had my full attention now.

"Yeah, like be my girl. You like me too, right?"

"Uh," I struggled for something to say besides 'you have a great smile.' "I think you're nice." *Oh that's lame.*

"Nice enough to go with?" Jason started to massage my back. It tickled a little and I tried hard not to laugh.

"Oh, you know, I'd like to…" Actually I didn't know for sure. I scrambled for something to say. He was still the cutest guy I'd ever seen, but all the input gave me goosebumps and I shivered—I was probably having an anxiety attack or something. *Concentrate!* I was supposed to be helping Kelly, and going out with Jason wouldn't help her in the slightest. Of course, going out with him *would* really get her back for being so mean, but did I want to go there? Okay, a little. But I can't. That would be wrong to do to Jason. Guilt one, lust zero. "Dad won't let me date until next year," I told him. *Thank you, Cathy.*

"You're kidding," Jason seemed amazed. "But he let you come tonight."

"Well, he lets me come to group events, just no one-on-one." I'd become way too good a liar.

"Wow, that's a drag." Then he smiled. "But he's not here now." He leaned in. I knew I was going to be kissed. *Forget crystals and the power.* I pursed my lips. But it was Jason's shoe that made the first contact as he crushed the top of my bare foot. Pain shot up my leg and I slumped down far enough to get a real close view of his lips as they grazed my eyeball.

"Ouch!" I grabbed my eye with one hand and tried to check out my throbbing foot through blurry vision all while trying to look cool. *I'm pretty sure I failed.*

"Aw, man, I'm sorry," Jason stammered. "Are you all right? Was that your eye?"

"It's okay. It was probably my fault." I winced and pointed to the ladies room. "But I think I'll check it out in the light. " Just in case my eyeball popped out or something.

The small room was crowded with girls fixing each other's hair and makeup and talking about different guys. In an empty stall, I found a safe haven. The smallest two toes on my right foot were already turning red. Compared to the left foot, the swelling had begun. At least my eyeball was still in its socket.

Cathy knocked on the stall door.

"Julie? Are you in there?"

"Yeah, it's me."

"What happened? You two looked great and then you dashed away."

"Jason stepped on my foot."

"You're kidding," Cathy laughed. "Does it hurt?"

"What do you think?" I opened the door.

Cathy took one look and cracked up. "Did he step on your eye, too?"

"What do you mean?" I limped through the crowd to the mirror. My carefully applied eyeliner was now smeared up to my right eyebrow. "Oh no." I reached for a paper towel and began wiping my face. The left eye makeup had to go, too, since neither of us had brought a purse with extra makeup. "Let's get out of here. Poor Jason. He'll probably develop a complex and never try to kiss anyone ever again."

"I doubt that," Cathy laughed as we moved into the hallway, me limping, of course. "I know he likes you and I have one of my feelings. You haven't seen the last of his lips. You'd better get some goggles."

I wish that were true, but my chance was gone. We made it back to the gym. A fast song was blaring and kids were jumping and twisting all over the place. And I thought I needed dance lessons.

"Are you okay?" Jason asked. "Do you want to dance again?"

My foot throbbed out an answer only I could hear. "I don't think I can."

"Want me to sit with you?"

The familiar warmth of the crystal started at my neck. It grew hot to the touch—a strange contrast to the cool goosebumps rising up my arms. What did they mean this time? Over my shoulder I saw Eddie. He handed some cash to Randy. To my far left, a teacher watched.

"I'm sorry." *I really am.* "But I have to talk to Eddie."

In my fantasy world, he watched me walk away admiring my smoothness. But my foot hurt so bad I had to hop the last few steps. I grabbed Eddie's arm for support.

"What the…?" Eddie asked.

"Wanna dance?"

"Are you kidding?" Okay, so considering the picture I must have made hobbling over to him, it was probably a surprising question. He leaned close enough for me to tell he had shaved the four or five straggly hairs off his chin and whispered. "We're doing a little business right now."

"That's why I'm here. Don't look, but there's a teacher checking you guys out. Come sit with me and pretend to be talking." He glanced back at Randy for a second, then helped me back to my chair next to some big floral arrangement just as Mr. Carpenter reached Randy. As soon as I sat down, a sprig of baby's breath poked me in my good eye.

Kelly, clutching a red rose Valentine's bouquet, swooped in and waved her bouquet in my face.

"Don't get too used to being with Jason," Kelly said. "He and the guys have a little contest where they pick out a new girl each year. I guess you're this year's little target."

What? How had I managed to land on Planet of the Witch?

"What did you say?" Cathy asked with a look that screamed, 'I want to smack you in the head.' Cathy straightened her back, which pushed her new B cups higher.

Kelly's date stared directed at Cathy. "Wow. You look great," he ogled. Kelly hit him in the ribs with her elbow. Apparently her date wasn't supposed to notice anyone else.

"Let it go, Cathy." I pulled her back while fighting my own urge to pounce on Kelly.

"That's right. Run and hide, you losers."

Full of anger, I didn't want to leave as much as I wanted to tear out Kelly's hair, one handful at a time. Just as the image of dragging her around the room by what would be left of her hair raced through my mind, the flowers hit the floor. Actually, just the petals. All of them. Kelly now held on a bouquet of stems. A pile of red and white covered her feet.

"What?" Kelly cried. "How did..."

I tried to stand up and felt a hand on my elbow. It was Eddie. Oh yeah...I'd forgotten he was there.

"That was cool," he said as he pulled me a few seats away.

"What?"

"The flowers," he whispered. "How'd you break them apart like that?"

"I don't know what you're talking about."

"Oh come on. It's not like I haven't seen you do something like this before. Things seem to happen to Kelly when you're around. Like when her Halloween costume flooded, and when the soda cup seemed to spill by itself. Anytime Kelly's being a jerk and you're around, something happens to her. What are you? Telekinetic or something?"

"Get real," were the two words that came out of my mouth. But two different words were going through my head: *Oh crap!*

Chapter 28

Four hours later, my butt was on my desk chair, my foot rested on the edge of my bed wrapped in an icepack and I was still trying to figure out why of all people it would be Eddie who would figure out I was a freak.

The red glow of the digital clock stared at me and I waited for the time to advance to seven a.m. in New Orleans. Five more minutes and Gramma's alarm would go off. I knew better than to her wake up—only her Elvis Presley alarm clock had that honor.

In my left hand was the cordless phone. In my right hand I held a pencil which I drummed on the notepad I had used to write down all the strange things that had happened to Kelly.

"I'm sure she's just accident prone," I tested my theory out loud. No one in the empty room disagreed. "But…I do remember there were a lot of goosebumps. Maybe it's been here all along and I've been ignoring it?"

Four more minutes. I drummed faster and faster until the pencil slipped from my fingers and landed on the floor. Telekinetic? I stared at it, swallowed hard, and then said, "Come."

Nothing. My imagination has been working overtime. I looked longingly at my bed, then back at the clock. Three more minutes. I yawned and rubbed my eyes. My attention returned to the pencil and a vision of a thin clear thread between it and my mind appeared. When I pulled on the thread, the pencil wiggled.

"Ah!" I slapped a hand over my mouth and listened to see if Dad woke up. It was silent upstairs. The clock tripped over and I entered Gramma's number.

"Hello," cracked Gramma's morning voice.

"Help!"

"Honey, what's wrong?"

"Things are moving around me."

"You mean you're making progress with your powers?"

"No. I mean things are actually, literally, moving. As in, can you spell telekinetic?"

"Are you kidding?"

"Kidding? I'm not sure I even have a sense of humor anymore."

"Hang on. Let me run downstairs and wake up Rose. She's had some experience with this."

I grabbed the pencil and stuffed it into the drawer.

"We're both on the phone," Rose said. "Tell us everything."

From the costume malfunction to the decapitation of the rose bouquet to the pencil, I rushed through the events before taking a breath. The phone was silent. "Are you still there?" I asked.

"We're here," Rose said. "I'm just trying to put this together. It's not unheard of for a third generation Changer to have multiple powers. I'm a third just like you. But I am surprised that you can read crystals and move objects—each take so much energy. There's only one answer. There must be another force involved."

"Oh, great. Now my life sounds like a Star Wars remake."

Rose ignored me. "Someone with ties to Three Rivers was in Sonoma sometime in the past and left behind energy. It's the only explanation."

"Maybe it was Mom? I mean I've felt really connected to Sonoma. More than any other placed I've lived. There has to be something to it."

"I don't think so," Gramma said. "Marina and I were only there one day. I can't imagine what she could have done that quickly. Besides she was so young. What could she have done?"

"Whoever it was," Rose added, "your powers are feeding off the energy and growing."

"Like aliens?"

"See, Rose," Gramma said. "I told you, she watches too many movies."

"This is remarkable, Julie," Rose continued. "Your powers will always be strong, but as long as you stay in Sonoma near this force, there's no telling how intense they will become. This is a great gift for a Changer."

"Yeah, great," I mumbled.

"I want you to spend some time with us in New Orleans this summer," Rose said. "I can help you. In the meantime, be calm. Telekinesis reacts spontaneously during times of strong emotion until you learn how to handle it through practice. Avoid drama."

Avoid drama? Get real. I'm sixteen. My whole life is drama.

"Are you listening, Julie?"

"Yes, Gramma, I'm listening. I'm a new mind-reading, telekinetic freak and I have to calm down so I can practice to be a better freak. I heard it all. What am I supposed to do now?"

Chapter 29

Monday morning, my bruised foot looked much worse than it felt—I was hardly limping. I started to put on one of my new outfits, and then decided I'd rather wear something old and comfy. I talked Dad into giving me a ride to school.

"Hey, Julie, how's the foot?" I recognized the tall blond guy from my Spanish class walking over to me as I made my way across the parking lot. I didn't know his name. How did he know mine? There must be another Julie with a sore foot in the quad.

"How's the foot?" he repeated, blocking my path to the main hallway.

"Uh, okay." After a long pause I realized he was expecting conversation. "You're in my Spanish class, right?"

"Yeah." He smiled. "I heard about your foot and wanted to make sure you were all right."

"Oh, thanks. I'm fine." Thankfully the first bells were ringing. "I have to go. I don't want to be late for class."

"Do you need some help?" He was still smiling.

"No, thanks. I'll be okay."

"You're sure? All right then. See you later, babe."

Babe? "Yeah… bye."

The tardy bells were ringing by the time I reached class. Everyone watched me enter the room. The attention made me wish

I had worn my new outfit and dried my hair instead of pulling it back into a wet ponytail.

Several times during class I caught people staring at me. A few even whispered and pointed. *What is up with them?* I couldn't concentrate on anything when Ms. Donovan assigned a book to read and handed out copies at the end of class, I just stuffed it into my crammed backpack and hurried off to the library.

During the break period, Cathy tracked me down at the back corner table in the library. "I ran all the way here," Cathy panted and adjusted her bra strap. "I can't believe how stupid people can be. Imagine thinking you were in the middle of a love triangle."

"What?" I winced when I tried to stand up too fast. "I knew something was going on."

"You didn't hear? The word is Jason and Eddie were fighting over you at the dance. You tried to break it up and ended up with a black eye and a broken foot. Oh yeah—and Eddie didn't get caught with pot because you were holding it for him."

I don't believe this! A slow sigh came from my throat as I covered my face with my hands. "How do these things happen to me?" I held my hands to my cheeks and pressed hard enough to pucker my lips into a fish shape. "How could anyone come up with that?"

"Well, I heard that Kelly heard Eddie ask you to dance and then Jason said no and when you guys were dancing Eddie stalked around you two and then Eddie and Jason started fighting and you got caught in the middle." Cathy stopped to take a breath. "You know it's really kind of romantic. I wish two guys were fighting over me."

"Hello, Cathy, anyone in there?" I tapped Cathy's forehead. "You know that's not what happened."

"Oh yeah, I know." Cathy looked a little disappointed. "If you won't let me smack Kelly in the head, let's call her on her lies right now in front of everyone. She's right over there."

"Shh!" I hushed her. Jason walked by. He smiled and waved, but thankfully (I think) took no for an answer. On the other hand—why did he give up so easy on me? *No drama my foot. Literally.*

Kelly sat on the edge of the display table, holding a small cup of soda down at her side, away from view of the librarian.

"What's the matter, Julie?" Kelly said as Cathy and I walked up to her. "Having a tough day?" She laughed. Of course. I wanted to explode her drink then and there. But when I focused my anger on the cup, nothing happened. To the cup that is. I did manage to knock over the entire display of books.

The librarian rushed over and stood at the pile on the floor like she was giving them last rites. "This is why you are not supposed to sit on the tables, Kelly! And a drink? Thank heaven that didn't spill." She took the cup from Kelly, holding it by her fingertips to avoid contamination, then dropped it into a trashcan. "Now help me set these back up."

My powers may not have been accurate, but they were satisfying. I couldn't have the first kiss the way I wanted it, but that doesn't mean I have to be afraid of her anymore.

Chapter 30

The button on my jeans cut into my stomach as I bent to pull the take out box still filled with chow mein from the bottom shelf of the refrigerator. I'd been burying the loss of my first kiss under piles of food all week. I'd have to get over it and move on soon. The kitchen was about empty anyway.

Dad came in and hung the phone back onto the cradle as the microwave dinged. When the entire wall mounted unit dropped to the floor, We stared at the plastic box hanging by a single wire for a moment.

"I'll call Ms. Donovan," I said. "From my cell."

"No," he said quickly. "I'll fix it."

He really didn't want to see her if he was actually going to fix something himself.

"Aurora's coming tomorrow."

"Really!" I squealed, feeling better already. I wasn't even interested in the sticky noodles anymore. "That's so great. What's bringing her here early?

"I called her and asked if she could come early for her visit to stay with you while I'm gone. I have an interview in Laramie, Wyoming, for two projects that should see us through the year—"

"Wyoming!" Where was that? Far from Sonoma, I'd bet.

"There's nothing I can do. We have to go where the work is. The economy's so bad; it's hard to find anyone willing to spend money on municipal art projects." He stood and waited for my response.

I had none. What was there to say? Wyoming?

"This sucks." I groaned and stuffed a mouthful of chow mein into my mouth. The two mountainous piles of books, notes, and binders were divided on my desk—to the left, homework due soon; to the right, homework already late. There was no way I would be able to finish everything. I could push off geometry again. It wouldn't be collected until next week. The sooner I can get out of school, I can be on my own and choose my own place to live. But two and a half years seemed like a long time.

My telekinesis was growing more accurate as I found new ways to procrastinate by elevating my Spanish book from one pile to the other.

"I'm so far behind, I don't know where to start," I told the stacks. And then there was the powers crap. Dad and Kelly still baffled me, but Eddie wasn't hard to figure out. With everything he was doing for his mother, it was hard to label him a loser. But he was so mad at his dad, he couldn't let it go.

Not that figuring him out helped me know what to do. It's like he was standing on the edge of something big and I didn't know which side he'd go. And I'll have to be extra careful around him now. He can't find out about my powers—no one can.

I switched my telekinetic attention to the little book Ms. Donovan had assigned: "The Valley of the Moon," by Jack London.

"Wait a minute!" I tilted it on an angle and read the cover for the first time. This was the same book that Mom had read and that had pulled her to Sonoma.

It helped that "Valley of the Moon" was a thin novel and wouldn't take me too long. I climbed into bed. The covers felt the kind of great that only comes on a day that combined clean sheets with just-shaved legs. I cuddled into the softness, balanced the take out box between my knees and turned to page one.

It began oddly. The main character, Saxon, was living in the Bay Area during the Great Depression and she was waiting for her husband to be released from jail for trying to start a union. Then they traveled hundreds of miles by foot to find the home she imagined in her heart and ultimately found it in Sonoma Valley.

The back cover of the book told how Jack London had lived and written in a small house in the hills above Sonoma. His large dream home The Wolf House burned down just before it was finished and the ruins still remain.

Saxon had been right about Sonoma. I'd spent enough time in U-hauls and new cities to know that. "You loved Sonoma, too," I said to Mom's picture on the desk. "How am I going to convince Dad?"

Cathy leaned across the sticky table in the quad the next day and whispered, "so, Thomas called me again last night." The buttons on her jacket strained across her growing breasts. "He asked me a lot of homework questions, but I know he gets better grades than I do. Obviously he likes me. I don't know what to do, though. I mean I liked him at the beginning of school, and then we became friends. But he is cute."

"I don't know either. I don't have a lot of experience. But there is something I wanted to talk to you about." Once I told Cathy, the move would be real. "Dad left today on a job interview."

"Left? To where?"

"Laramie, Wyoming. A rodeo mural."

"Wyoming! No! He can't do this to us. We have to stop him. There must be a way to keep him here. I know—we should find him a job."

"The problem isn't just having a job. He can't stand to stay in one place long. He doesn't like becoming attached."

"Well there must be something we can do. We need to focus all of our positive energy on a solution." Cathy's voice rose. She pounded her fist on the table and the button holding her jacket closed across her chest popped off and landed in my burrito.

"Whoa!" I picked out the miniature Frisbee and handed it back. "Are we growing again?"

"No way! I'm staying a B—and you're staying in Sonoma!"

The white rental car parked in front of my house at the end of the school day lifted my spirits. When Gramma stepped out of the front door and met me on the porch, I dissolved into a blubbery nine-year-old mess.

"I can't move to Wyoming!"

After several minutes, Gramma reached into her sweater pocket for a tissue and handed it to me, pulling me inside to the living room.

"I've never felt so connected anywhere before," I choked. "There's something I get from living here and I don't want to give it up. I know it sounds strange, but I feel like Mom wants me to be here."

"I've been thinking a lot about the force that's given you so much strength here. I've been wondering if it came from Marina. But we were here for only a day and we were together pretty much all of the time except for that short hike in Jack London Park."

"We never went up there, Gramma. I just read the same book Mom did before she went."

"I can't imagine anything she could have done that would have created this force in that quick trip."

It was hard for me not to imagine anything.

I bent over with my elbows on my knees and rested my head in my hands, rubbing my forehead. Sonoma had become a home for me. Maybe what worked for me could work for Dad.

"Hey, how about a friend? Or a date? Maybe we can get Dad together with Ms. Donovan. She seems to like him, for some reason."

"I don't think that would be fair to her," Gramma said. "I love him, but he's an emotional mess. He can't move forward until he's dealt with the past."

What else? "Having my boxes unpacked made the house feel like a home to me. What a relief it was not to have the stacks hanging over me like little coffins of my past."

"He has lots of empty built-in shelves in his room. We could unpack for him," Gramma said. "He'll have to deal with at least some of the stuff then. On the other hand, it would be a real invasion of his privacy."

"What's the worst that will happen? He'll be grouchy and moody? That's everyday."

"Well, all right. I'll help. Maybe if we put them out and make him face it, it might be the catalyst that will shock him back to life."

"Or make him run away even sooner." I was out of ideas. I had to take the chance.

Two days later, we moved his furniture back against the fresh blue walls. We tackled the boxes—mostly art and art history books. One contained framed pictures and a family album. I arranged the books and many of the pictures of Dad and Mom on his shelves. One of the photos showed the three of us when I was just a newborn. I framed it for his nightstand. For the first time since Mom died, all of the boxes were unpacked. I was moved in.

"The room looks fabulous," Gramma said, "and homey."

"I hope he likes it." I shivered.

"Yeah," Gramma said. "I'm counting on my age to protect me."

"I'm counting on you to protect me!"

That evening, Dad returned looking tired, depressed, and basically normal.

"How was the trip?" I asked. Crappy, I hoped.

"I won't hear for a few weeks. I was their first interview." I stood in the hallway not knowing how to say we'd been through all of his things. "What have you two been up to?"

"We had some time on our hands," Gramma said, "so Julie and I decided to finish moving in."

"In? Considering the circumstances wouldn't it be better to begin repacking some of this stuff?"

I took a deep breath and started in. "I know you have to follow your work, but for now I live here. And I want to feel like it—not count the days. I wanted you to feel it too, so I…I moved you in."

"You didn't!"

He marched upstairs. I raced behind him, followed by Gramma.

"Your room was so cold and empty," I stammered. "When mom was alive our house was always warm…a nice place to be. I wanted to have that again." I ran into his back when he stopped cold in the doorway.

Fear filled my stomach and goosebumps pushed against the skin on my arms, trying to get out. His pain seared into my heart like I'd been stuck with a pitch fork when he turned to face me. He held the picture that I had placed on the nightstand.

"It was my idea," Gramma said weakly. "We thought you'd like it. Julie worked hard to make something she thought you'd like. It's not a pressure to stay here. It's a gift for you to enjoy with the time you have here. It's…" Gramma stopped. He wasn't listening.

Dad seemed to notice me for the first time. The pain in my heart softened, but my stomach flipped.

"I can see you've gone through a lot of work and expense for me," Dad said slowly, like he was trying to pick his words carefully. "You shouldn't have done it, but I appreciate the effort."

That was the closest he was going to come to thanking us, because he didn't like it and I knew it. The painful memory of Mom's death was written in the lines around his eyes.

We moved aside as Dad left the room and closed his bedroom door. I knew that would be the last time he entered that room. I wasn't sure if I blamed him or not.

I sat at my window in a wash of light from the full moon. I needed help. I thought of Mom who had given everything she had to make sure her daughter was safe. And of the fictional Saxon who had kept her faith that she would find her Valley of the Moon. There had to be a way to get Dad to stay.

Chapter 31

My life went from depressing to 'oh-crap-haven't I got enough to deal with' when Ms. Donovan called me to her desk Tuesday.

"You didn't do very well on your midterm." Ms. Donovan passed the essay back to me with an F marked on it.

"Ugh!" I hadn't put much time into it, but I thought I'd be able to fake my way through it.

"Although I like your Valley of the Moon report, lately you haven't been doing your homework. Is there something going on I should know about?"

"No. I've just been busy." *Trying to hold my life together.*

"I checked your file in the office and see that your grades have taken a beating—well below where they were last semester. That's a sign to me it's time for a parent conference."

"Let's skip that," I pleaded. "I can do better. I'll try harder."

"I'd like to take your word for it, but sometimes I have to go with my gut instinct. I'll call your father and see what we can schedule."

In Science class, Kelly twisted around in her chair and grinned from behind Miss Day's back. *Another day with the devil*! Kelly whispered to Kevin, then interrupted Miss Day, who had been writing on the board.

"Miss Day?"

"Yes, Kelly?"

"Could you please ask Julie to be quiet again? I can't concentrate with all her whispering."

My mouth fell open. I found myself so often in this position lately that my tongue was always dry and stuck to the roof of my mouth.

"Do I need to send you out?" Miss Day asked me.

"Uh, no." I tried to sink lower in the plastic molded seat and almost slipped out.

When Miss Day turned back to the board, I saw Kevin give Kelly a quiet high five. Giving up Jason wasn't enough for her, huh?

Cold wind blew through my sweater but I still took the long way around the Plaza Park on my way home. I hoped today was one of the days Dad was so engrossed in work that he wouldn't hear the phone ring.

No such luck. He was waiting for me in the kitchen. "I was right in the middle of my work today," he said, "and I had to stop because I got a call from Ms. Donovan. She wants to see us at four thirty. What's going on?"

"Nothing. I've just been so busy. I guess I let a few things slip."

"That doesn't sound like such a big deal to me. I resent being summoned to the school like I've done something wrong."

He just didn't want to see her and act like an idiot again. "She's not a bad teacher." Ms. Donovan was great, but I didn't think he'd take my word for it. And even though I didn't want to go to this conference either, I didn't want Dad to hate her.

"We'll see about that."

Judging from the way the speed of his tapping foot increased as we were forced to wait in the hallway, Dad's anger was growing. The janitor was cleaning the water fountain next to us and the smell of the disinfectant was strong. But I didn't want to budge. Here had to be better than what was waiting behind the door. I'd never been in trouble at school before. At 4:40, Ms. Donovan called us in as she opened the door to let a grim-looking mother and father out, followed by a red-faced guy I recognized from class.

"I'm sorry you had to wait, Drew," Ms. Donovan said, holding out her hand. "I'm afraid we ran a little long. Everything okay with the house?"

"Yes." Dad sailed past her without shaking her hand. "Could we get right to this? I have to get back to work."

"All right then," Ms. Donovan's smile faded. "I saw from Julie's cumulative file this is her seventh school in seven years."

"I go where the work is. This year I'm in Sonoma. Next year may be Wyoming."

Ms. Donovan squeezed her lips together and paused. "Julie, would you mind waiting in the hallway. I'd like to speak with your father alone."

I moved back to the hallway, then leaned close to the door to listen. "That must be hard on your daughter, always having to make new friends."

"She's all right so far. Aren't we here to talk about her schoolwork?"

"Yes. I find when a good student's grades suddenly drop, there's usually something going wrong with her friends or at home. Now I know Julie's circle of friends and they're doing fine, so…"

"So what you're implying is something is going wrong at home?"

Whoa Dad! It wasn't like him to dislike someone so much. Except Eddie, of course. I tried to peek through a crack in the door.

"I don't need anyone, especially someone without kids, telling me how to raise my daughter. If something's wrong it's probably that Eddie kid that's been hanging around."

"Now, Drew, please don't be upset. I'm not implying anything. I just want to know why Julie's grades have changed. When this happens I ask myself questions like: Does she have a quiet place to work? Does she do her homework regularly? Is she eating well? Getting enough sleep? Is there something I or her parents can do to help?"

Dad's voice calmed. "I work long hours. Julie takes care of herself and she's always done fine."

"Yes, but since she's only sixteen, I imagine you are keeping an eye on her so she stays on the right track."

"Sure I do. Are we finished?"

"Not just yet. I need to see Julie's grades go up. I'm sorry to hear she'll be moving to a new school again this September. It can be difficult to fit into a new high school, especially for a girl her age. It looks likes she's starting to find a niche here. Let me read you a paragraph from her book report on The Valley of the Moon." There was a pause, then came the words I'd written in my report: "I understand how Saxon felt as she searched for her special valley. I feel like I've been doing the same thing for seven years, but instead of a bedroll and ukulele, I travel by U-Haul. Though I'll probably move on again, a piece of this valley will stay with me and when I'm able, I'll return."

Through the small opening in the doorway, I could see Dad's back straighten. "I have to go where the work is."

"I understand. I see you stayed in New Orleans for several years. Do you mind my asking what you did then?"

"I was a teacher. I taught art at the high school and the local junior college."

I heard the sound of his steps just in time to avoid being hit in the nose by the swinging door. "If there's nothing else, I have to get back to work."

"I guess that's it." Ms. Donovan looked to me. "If your grades don't go up, you're going to have to go through summer school—either here or in…where was it? Wyoming?"

"I'll try to do better." I looked at the floorboard for a hole to crawl into. Dad looked so mad; he would probably want to leave before school was even out. I followed him out to the car.

"That woman had some nerve telling me what to do," he said. He started the engine.

"She was only trying to help." I was really glad I hadn't tried to set them up. For her sake.

"She exaggerated about you, didn't she?" He faced me, which made me uncomfortable. I wasn't used to having his direct attention. "It's not all that bad moving around, right? You get to make new friends and see new places.

I chewed my bottom lip, trying to think of something to say and trying not to think of anything.

"Uh!" Dad groaned.

He dropped me at the curb in front of our house and muttered something about going out and then drove off.

"Do you have to be such a jerk?" I said to the back of the car as he turned the corner.

I get that your kid getting in trouble at school is no fun for parents, but it isn't like I'd flooded the science lab by plugging up the sinks with paper towels or anything. And it is partly his fault!

Stamping up the wooden stairs into the house, I grew madder with each step. By the time I climbed up to my room I didn't want to collapse on my bed and calm down. I wanted to...I didn't know...but something.

Although he'd never said specifically to stay out of his studio, I felt like I was breaking some kind of rule as I walked through his doorway when he wasn't there. His mural was in several sections leaning against the walls, but I didn't bother with them. It was the easel in the corner that pulled me forward.

That painting gets him so bent out of shape every time he sits there. What if I hid it from him and say someone stole it? That would be lame. Dad wasn't exactly Picasso. I held the corners of the canvas cover.

This might be an important piece that helps me figure him out or maybe just some really embarrassing picture I wished I'd never seen.

I held my breath and lifted the dust cloth.

"Mom!" I said in one long exhale.

The long brown hair, the small, rounded jaw—the painting was Mom, I was sure. But there were no eyes or mouth. From the thickness of the oil paint, it looked as though Dad had been painting and repainting the face, trying to get it right, then covering it up again.

Torture. I recovered Mom's unfinished face and slumped out. *Now I know what it's like to not want to enter a room again.*

Chapter 32

Senor Otero conjugated the verb "comer" on the wipe board. I was concentrating on what to eat—roast beef or burrito? My stomach growled loudly. Several students turned toward the noise. I turned around too, pretending it hadn't come from me. My stomach growled again, but this time no one noticed. A loud siren wailed outside.

The entire class rushed to the windows, peered down onto the courtyard, and talked at once. "Check it out!" "What happened?" "I bet Stevie dropped a stink bomb in Science again." "Nah, I bet it was a fight!"

Two paramedics wheeled a stretcher past the window toward the art building. The teacher called everyone back to their desks to finish his lecture. He had to be kidding. No one moved. Moments later, the stretcher was back, holding a large man. Vice Principal Santiago walked alongside holding an umbrella.

The quad buzzed with the news during lunch as the whole school tried to escape the drizzle by wedging under the overhang.

Cathy had already gathered the whole scoop, of course.

"Mr. Rush, the art teacher, had a heart attack. Eddie probably saved his life!" Cathy gushed when she ducked out of the rain.

"Eddie?"

"Yeah. He was the only one in the classroom with him—they were cleaning up the paintbrushes when Mr. Rush just collapsed. Eddie called the office and they came running. If he wasn't there, Mr. Rush probably would have died on the spot, alone. Can you believe it? Wouldn't that be so depressing? Well, we don't know for sure if he's going to make it, I guess, but without Eddie he wouldn't have had a chance."

And without Mr. Rush, Eddie doesn't have much of a chance, either. "I'll be right back."

After not finding Eddie in the quad I was relieved to see him talking to the principal in the main hall. They disappeared into the office before I had a chance to say anything.

From head lice prevention to college application deadlines, I'd read every notice on the bulletin board before he came back into the hall. I stepped in his path.

"Hey."

He nodded, his eyes red and swollen.

"Um…I heard about Mr. Rush and I was, well, wondering if you're okay."

"I'm all right." Eddie's voice was deep.

"Have you heard anything?"

"He's still in surgery."

"I'm sorry. I know this must be hard on you. I know how much you like his class."

"He's like a dad…" Eddie choked then stopped, like he was sorry the words slipped out.

Mrs. Santiago came back into the hallway. "Eddie, please sign this form."

With Eddie's attention on getting his shaking hand to calm enough to write his name, I searched his thoughts.

How are you really, Eddie?

When we were alone again he turned and waited for me to say something. Inside I screamed 'Stay away from Randy! Make peace with your dad!' But after a long silence, which didn't do anything to alleviate my goosebumps, he said goodbye.

Crap!

I wish I could really talk to Mom—ask her what it was like when her powers were making her so miserable. I used to just talk to Mom's pictures. My new habit was rubbing the corners of her pictures to try to get her attention. The picture taken when she was visiting Sonoma was my favorite.

"I don't know what to do about Eddie or Dad," I said to the paper square. "You looked so happy. What was your secret?" Of course she didn't answer me. That would make my life easy. And nothing has been easy for me.

The depression that pulled Eddie down, took me with him.

Although I avoided looking at the piles of homework, I sensed they knew I was back and eagerly awaited which subject would be completed first. But even after the awful meeting with Ms. Donovan, I couldn't clear my mind of other peoples' troubles long enough to focus on school work.

Locking the door I set up the crystals and the rainbow pattern began its familiar dance on the ceiling. Someone laughed. Giggled, really.

Mom's sixteen-year-old face appeared. The picture I had carried all day came to life and Mom beckoned with a wave of her hand.

She stopped and turned, waiting. I drew forward into the vision, so near I reached out my hand to touch her, but just as I was close enough, she giggled again and ran to the head of a dirt path. Lined on each side by waist-high grass, it twisted around trees and shrubs.

Each time I came close, Mom would laugh and run further and further up. The wind blowing from my back, I followed as the trail climbed. "Stop!" I yelled, although all I heard was her giggling. The sun dropped suddenly, blanketing the path in shadows. Near the top, Mom disappeared around a corner. When I reached the bend, I stood alone in a clearing. "Mom? Mom!"

The last bit of sunlight dropped away. No sound and no sight except the moon above—yellow and warming my cold skin.

The vision dissolved. Mom was frozen and silent in the picture I still held.

"What were you leading me to?" *How was this vision supposed to help?* "Answer me!"

I flung the photo at my desk in anger, but when it slipped off the edge onto the floor I grabbed it back. I wasn't really angry. This vision may have left me with more questions, but it also left me feeling warm and closer to Mom than I have in a long time.

I wasn't really worried when Eddie didn't show up for English. If it had been me, I'd be taking a few days off, too. But by the time I finally saw him again sitting on the wet ground by a trashcan a week later my heart dropped into my stomach.

He was flipping the pages through his sketchbook, nearly ripping with each harsh page turn.

I marched up, ready to give him a pep talk—only to stop short at the sight of silver skulls in each of his earlobes. Earrings? When did he pierce his ears? And skulls? Like that's not depressing.

I'm in way over my head here! I started to turn then caught myself. Stupid powers. I was powerless. But I could use a heads up. I focused on the skull nesting in his red, swollen lobe. He swore and ripped a page from his sketchbook without noticing me. *What's the matter Eddie?*

I'll show her. First thing goes wrong and he'll run out again. I'll find Randy. I'm not going back into that house until he leaves, even if it takes all night.

His thoughts cleared as he looked up. "What do you want?"

"I'm sorry about Mr. Rush." I blurted.

"Why are you sorry? You didn't kill him."

"Uh…" *How could I respond to that?* "I know. Neither did you. At least you were there with him."

Eddie looked at me then like he'd never done before. I'd seen him annoyed with me, amused by me, and crushing on me. This time he obviously thought I was the stupidest person he'd ever met in his life. "Like that made any difference," he said slowly.

"Hey! I'm just trying to help."

Randy yelled out from the parking lot.

"I hear you! Quit yelling!" Eddie stood, forcing me back a few steps. "Don't you have girlfriends to play with?" He stalked away, slowing only to slam his sketchbook into the trashcan.

"What are you doing? You can't throw that away." I rushed to the full can, not really wanting to reach in.

"I just did." He glared at me at me like he was daring me to say something else nice. I couldn't think of a thing. He turned and followed Randy.

I held my breath and reached in to pick out his book. Why did it have to be spaghetti day? I tucked it into my backpack before returning to Cathy.

"What's with him?" Cathy asked. "Mr. Jerk Stoner is back?"

"I don't know about jerk." I watched Randy's car cruise through the parking lot. "I mean, how would you feel if the only person in your life who really knew you just died?"

Car horns blared as Randy ripped right through the stop sign and into the busy street. The engine gunned. I couldn't see Eddie in the passenger seat, but I could clearly see his hand waving out the window, flipping off the world. Being a member of the world and the last person he talked to, I took that personally.

Chapter 33

The worn cardboard cover of Eddie's sketchbook felt soft in my hands as I pulled it from the same wooden box that hid Mom's diary. Torn between the desire to respect his privacy and the curiosity to peek inside, I hadn't turned a single page since its rescue from the garbage two days before.

Maybe I might discover a way to help Eddie, I rationalized. Or I'm just nosey.

I sat back on the bed, opened to the first page, and read, "If found return to Eddie Kekune. And stay out!" The pages were dated beginning last summer, a month before school started. The first pages held pencil drawings of his mother, sitting in a wicker chair, her face lined and weak but with a glow like an angel. I could see he loved her.

Lulled into the sweetness, I winced when I turned the page and saw a different face. It looked like Eddie, but older. His dad? The face was divided into two halves. One half smiled kindly while the other side was twisted into fear. Definitely not angelic.

Goosebumps sprang out as I turned the page. I didn't need the date to know the drawing was from my first day of school. I recognized the zit.

There were many other pictures of me. He'd captured my feelings from the loneliness on the first day of school to my joy over the Christmas tree, to my anger toward Kelly on Halloween.

And I worry about his privacy? No wonder he's always popping up where I am. He's following me.

The last drawing was Mr. Kekune—his face contorted into something evil. I placed the book back into the box.

"Julie," Dad called. I jumped off the bed, knocking the box to the floor. Without looking, I kicked it under the bed just as he peeked through the open bedroom door.

"What's up?" He held two large bags.

"Nothing. I was just reading," I said. "What'd you buy?"

"More paint supplies. I'm almost finished with the mural. How about we walk over for some fish and chips in about an hour?"

"Okay." We may be leaving and he may be miserable, but at least he was talking to me again.

I closed the door and waited to hear him climb the attic steps. I reached under the bed to retrieve the box and it fell apart in my hands—not really broken, more like unassembled. It had been built in sections. "This is so cool." The purple felt tray revealed a false bottom.

Inside rested a small tissue-wrapped ball. The goosebumps tingled over my arms, the hair on the back of my neck stood up and a large lump began to grow in my throat. This had to be the fifth crystal.

My heartbeat increased as I unwound the tissue layers to reveal a small campfire-shaped crystal only about two inches wide. Flames licked up to sharp points. I moved as if in a trance to the window where the other crystals sat. The waning sunlight caught in all five crystals and began swirling into a vision. The circular rainbow formed into a porthole and the vision cleared.

It was a funeral.

Although my muscles hadn't moved, I was pulled forward to the casket like being dragged through a deep freezer—cold and dark, a place I'd never want to go. I tried to close my eyes but I was pulled closer and closer and then I saw the blond hair, so neatly combed into place I almost didn't know him.

Eddie.

His sketchbook lay under his folded hands. My legs gave out from under me and the vision vanished.

I found myself on the floor next to the bed. The sun had dropped below the hills and the crystals no longer glowed. I checked the clock. A half hour had passed. My rubbery legs weakened as I tried to stand. Covered in sweat, I stripped off my clothes and climbed into the shower. The warmth of the solid spray relieved my twitching muscles but the feeling of dread refused to wash away.

The last light from the setting sun through the window glowed red along the mountain's ridge, then disappeared into darkness. I turned on the light.

The flame-shaped crystal rested harmlessly on the sill and the box lay open on the floor. I placed the cold glass into the tray and pulled the box together.

Time to think. That's what I needed. Time to decide if I trusted what I thought I saw. If I did, Eddie was going to die.

The crisp night air was a welcome relief as I walked with Dad later down the cobblestone alley for popcorn chicken at Murphy's Irish Pub.

"You seem preoccupied," Dad said.

"Um, just school." How could I explain what was really going on? I didn't even know for sure.

"Just don't get me called into any more of those parent-teacher gripe-a-thons," Dad grimaced. "Especially that Donovan woman. And take the rent check to her tomorrow. I don't want to see her."

My feet froze in place. *I'm freaking out and he's whining that he had to be a parent for once?*

"It's not always about you!"

"What?" We faced off nose to nose. Or well, nose to second button on his shirt, but I wasn't going to back down.

"I won't let it get that bad again," I said.

The goosebumps rose on my arms before I heard skateboards coming up from behind us. The lump in my throat told me it was Eddie.

Three guys barreled pass. Randy first, then two others I didn't know. Eddie rolled up last. He stopped and picked up his board to walk past us.

"Your friends need to be more careful," Dad snapped at Eddie.

Eddie shrugged. I was still mad at the way he'd treated me, but I couldn't maintain eye contact. I'd seen him dead. I'd been caught peeking at something I shouldn't have. "Sorry," he said.

Randy called Eddie's name from the back parking lot. Eddie waved. "I gotta go. See ya." Eddie dropped his board and moved off.

I held my breath waiting for Dad to continue our argument.

"Those guys he's with look like trouble," Dad said and walked to the crowded restaurant where he took one of the outdoor tables under a heat lamp. I didn't say anything because for once I agreed with Dad. He didn't have to know it, though.

"I suppose you're going to tell me they're okay, too?" Dad continued.

"Well, no," I might as well tell him. "I think they're really losers. Eddie was doing okay, but then his art teacher Mr. Rush died of a heart attack and Eddie was the only one there to get help.

Now he's not so okay. And Eddie's Dad has been visiting the house."

"Visiting?"

"Yeah. I guess he freaked out when Eddie's mom got sick and took off. And now Eddie's hanging out with Randy and the other losers to get back at his Dad."

"You sure know a lot about him."

"Not really...It's just that Eddie's got a really bum deal. I hate to think what might happen."

"Take my advice and don't get involved." He picked up the menu and opened it, his face disappearing behind the laminated green pages. "It will only bring you down, too. Guys like Eddie can't be helped."

I propped my menu on the table and ducked behind it. I was beginning to think Dad was right about that, too.

We got back from dinner after nine and I ran straight for the kitchen phone.

"Who are you calling now?" Dad asked.

"I need to talk to Gramma." At least Gramma might understand what I'm going through.

"Wait until the morning. It's way too late to call tonight with the time difference," Dad said.

He was really overdoing the parenting thing tonight. "But I really need to talk to her about something." Fine, I would just use my cell phone as soon as I was in my room.

"Come on, Julie." He sat at the table and opened the paper. "It's not like it's life or death."

Chapter 34

Clouds covered the sky the next morning giving me a break from Gramma's advice: Do it again. Try to get the vision back. Great! I went down to the kitchen where Dad was attempting a knot in the only tie he owned.

"What's that for?" I asked.

"The council is unveiling my mural today to kick start tonight's festival in the Plaza and they want to take my picture."

"How come you didn't tell me?"

"It's not a big deal. You don't usually go to these things."

You don't usually tell me about them.

He made a growling noise in his throat but didn't say anything.

I helped him with the tie, but felt like the knot was really against my throat. I'd never gone to his other openings. I should go. A normal family would be there for big moments. I couldn't do much here anyway. "I'll go."

"You don't have to."

"No, I want to go. Really. Give me a second." I ran upstairs and grabbed my jacket and a brush, which I ran through my hair on the way back down the stairs.

We drove in silence around the Plaza. A crowd was waiting under an awning. Someone called Dad to the top and I held back. I didn't see anyone I knew except—*oh great*—Kelly.

She was standing next to a man with a city council badge. Her dad, I bet. A woman I guessed was Kelly's mom stood beside him with one hand on her husband's arm and the other holding a cell phone to her ear.

After speeches by the Arts Guild and the mayor, the large white cloth was dropped and the crowd made its way into the entry. Dad looked pleased. Like he knew he had done a good job. I wished it would last.

I hung back and followed after most of the people had already gone through. I pulled the zipper of my jacket up higher against the chilly air. Thanks to a breeze, I managed to tangle up my hair in the metal teeth. It hurt when several strands decided to stay attached to my jacket instead of my head. I shook my hair back to avoid doing it again and went inside. It was the first time I'd seen all the pieces together.

Set in a series of large canvasses, the mural showed children playing hide and seek in a vineyard thick with leaves and heavy with deep purple fruit.

One little girl in the painting—the only one not watching for the seeker—grabbed my attention. She was lifting a grape to her already purple mouth, smiling in utter happiness. Her sticky grape-covered face was more than familiar. It was my face at about six. My throat tightened. I'd always believed Dad never thought of anything but his work. And yet he had made me a part of it.

"I see you found her," Dad said as he came up beside me.

"Is she . . . me?"

He nodded, his face softening a bit. I think he almost smiled. "Yes."

"But...she looks so happy. Did I every really look like that?"

"Yes. Before." His voice cracked, then his face hardened back to the usual stone. He turned his back on the mural. "I need to stay a few minutes for the reception and then we can go."

I watched him walk to the mayor, who clapped him on the back and pulled him over to Kelly's parents. Kelly's mom was carrying the largest black brief case I'd ever seen with gold clasps that meant something about a designer. I studied the mural again. Dad had really done a great job. *I'm proud of him.* And for a brief moment there, when the mayor first unveiled the mural, there was a flash of pride on Dad's face, too, I knew it. That was a change. He really could make a place in Sonoma.

Too bad he couldn't see it.

"So, your dad's an artist." I had been so lost in thought I hadn't heard Kelly come up beside me.

"Yeah," I turned to face her, ready for the crap she was sure to start.

Kelly smiled, like she'd just beat me at Monopoly and then turned and walked away.

What was that about? I turned back to the mural and waited for Dad to finish.

We ran back through the fresh sprinkles of rain to the car. Once we shut out the weather, I felt Dad relax and peeked into his mind. *This is a good town. If I was a better father, I could give it to her.*

I nearly choked. He was actually thinking of me. I blurted out, "What are you thinking about?"

"Oh, what Ms. Donovan said." He chewed on his lip a bit as gripped the wheel. "I can see that all this moving has been hard on you. I . . . I don't know, I just kind of wish we could stay, for you. But I just don't know how. This is the best I can do right now."

"I know," I whispered. At that moment I knew I'd never go live with Gramma. I couldn't leave him alone.

The sun broke through the clouds for a moment just before sunset. I set up the crystals and relaxed against my pillows. Nothing happened.

Sunlight was coming through the dolphin, the campfire, and the crescent moon. I held onto the doorknob. *What's wrong?* I looked down at the crystal necklace I wore everyday, but it wasn't there. I threw myself on the floor and crawled around to each corner and under my bed. But no necklace. "Calm down and focus!" I leaned against my bed, picked off the dust bunnies that hung to the ends of my hair, and retraced my steps. I remembered having it on this morning. And at the Plaza didn't I have it on…? "Uh!" It must have come off when I caught my hair in my jacket zipper!

I can't lose mom's necklace! How am I going to save Eddie now?

I ran back through the drizzle to city hall and searched the entire area. But it wasn't there. It wasn't anywhere. And it was getting dark.

Dropping down on the wet curb I put my face in my hands. *Where is it? What happened to it?*

I froze. I knew.

Kelly.

Chapter 35

Pulling my head out of the garbage can the next morning, I cursed Kelly. The plaza janitor said lost and found was empty, but he'd dumped his dustpan into this barrel. It wasn't there. *I know Kelly has it. How am I going to get it back?*

Eddie beat me to English. He slouched low with his head propped up by his hand. He looked exhausted. But at least he was here and safe. For now.

Kelly sat in front of him. Her purse hung on the back of the chair. *Was my necklace in there?* I wanted to demand she return it, but accusing her of stealing in front of the class wasn't going to get my crystal back.

Ms. Donovan was reading poems to the class. Poetry was my favorite section, but the most poetic thing on my brain was 'Kelly is a thief. I want to punch her in the teeth.'

The small leather bag had a zipper closure with a wooden palm tree hanging off the end. Maybe my powers can help. If I spill her purse on the floor, at least I'll know if it's in there. I concentrated on the palm tree and visualized a thin thread attached to its trunk. I gave the thread a short tug to the right and it unzipped a bit. Loudly. Kelly whipped her head around at the sound, tucked her purse on her lap and glared at Eddie.

He held his hands up in the air and shook his head. Kelly squinted at me before turning around. Shocked by the world's loudest zipper, it was hard to look innocent.

The first rule to espionage must be to act natural. Wish I'd known that before I decided to sit right behind Kelly in keyboarding instead of across the room. She took one look at me and moved her purse to her lap. How insulting! I only wanted to steal back what was already mine.

Our class assignment: to use a spreadsheet to create of list of the ten things we'd change about our lives. My list was easy. I typed "stay in Sonoma" on all ten lines.

We were supposed to send a copy to the printer when finished. Maybe if I can get Kelly up, I can get to her purse.

I sat up on one knee and leaned forward to see Kelly's keyboard. As she typed I concentrated on her mouse until it moved off the side of the desk, dangling by the short cord. She grabbed the mouse and moved it back to continue typing. She stopped briefly to crack her knuckles and I moved the mouse again to the print key and tapped several times.

"Oh!" Kelly cried. "I wasn't going to send that!"

She ran to the printer—with her purse. So untrusting. She grabbed each copy as it came out and held them to her chest.

No wonder…I looked at her screen. Number one on her list: Parents who care about her more than work. Number two: Family vacations instead of summer camp. Number three: Jason as a boyfriend. I couldn't read the rest before she sat back down and stuffed the pages into her backpack. She didn't see me watching as she deleted her list and began again. Better grades was now number one. Better than straight A's? How's that going to happen?

Our regular table was too far off to the side for a clear view of the purse. Eddie's spot was good, though. He sat on the ground with his back against the Foods building.

"Why are you staring at Eddie?" Cathy whispered. "You aren't starting to like him or something are you?"

"Not even remotely possible." Even with the vision I was still pissed at him for blowing me off the other day. But I needed to see into that purse. "I'm just trying to figure him out, that's all."

"He has gotten pretty weird lately. He hasn't said a word to me all week."

"I think I'll go talk to him and see what's wrong."

"Want me to come, too?"

"I'm good." I couldn't tell her that from where Eddie sat, I'd probably be able to see into Kelly's bag. Kill two birds with one purse.

Eddie barely looked at me as I walked up.

"Hey." I decided to pretend we were still friends. "We're going out for pizza after school. Want to come along?"

"No," he sighed.

I tried to pretend that wasn't annoying. "You haven't been around much lately."

"I've been busy."

I nodded. I didn't know why. The purse was in clear view. *Now or never.* One tug opened the zipper and another dropped the whole thing on the ground upside down with enough force to send the contents flying.

Kelly's wallet dropped with a thud at her feet, four tubes of lip-gloss scattered, one tampon rolled under the table, and my crystal necklace landed halfway between us. I stepped up quickly but she grabbed it first.

"Hey!" she screeched, jumping to her feet and looking like she'd claw my eyes out.

"That's mine." I must have yelled, because suddenly the entire quad was watching us.

"Prove it."

"It's one-of-a-kind. It was made for my mom." Was it my imagination or were people starting to circle around us?

Kelly must have felt it, too, because when she spoke she was really looking around. Not at me.

"How do I know it's yours? It looks valuable. I think it should be turned in. Don't worry, if it's really yours, you'll get it back. Eventually."

I couldn't wait. Neither could Eddie.

"It's mine." The crowd pushed me forward. I grabbed the broken chain, but she still held the crystal. I don't know if she wanted to be or if the crowd pushed her, but suddenly we were nose to nose. *Okay—my nose, her neck.*

What's with people? Why would they want to see me fight? I wasn't sure if she was going to hit me or what, but being close enough to see that she didn't even have any tiny pimples really pissed me off.

"It's Julie's necklace." Jason's voice came from behind me. "She wears that thing every day."

He came to my rescue? Kelly's lower lip quivered and the spark of anger I'd seen in her eyes was gone. She released the crystal. When she looked at me the anger returned. Without another word, she turned to pick up the rest of her purse contents. Except the tampon.

Kelly pushed through the crowd so hard, one girl landed on her butt. *I wish I could do that to her. Where's a banana peel when you need one?* A soda can gleamed near her path. I moved it under her feet just in time to trip her up. She fell face first onto the ground. But not before hitting on the edge of the table with enough force that it sounded like someone was playing baseball with an overripe cantaloupe.

Blood covered her mouth and nose. I couldn't see her front teeth. She was white everywhere there wasn't blood.

"Oh!" Cathy cried as she came up beside me and squeezed my arm. "Even I feel sorry for her."

What have I done? My fingers grabbed at the backspace key on my bracelet and I pulled.

A strong wind blew dust into my face and I stumbled backwards. When I opened my eyes, I sat flat on the floor next to my seat in keyboarding and Kelly's pages were spitting out of the printer. *Jeez, that was a ride!* I jumped up into my seat and watched Kelly frantically grabbing each sheet of paper. Seeing her perfect little un-smashed face actually made me smile. *Now I know how to help her.*

Satisfied that she'd collected all the pages Kelly headed back to her seat, but not before I pressed print one more time.

I sent my own list next and walked over to the printer and collected both copies.

"What needs to be changed in my life, by Kelly Alazar." Wind blew me back to the unveiling of Dad's mural and I found myself landing hard behind Kelly's mom. *This backspace crap is going to break every bone in my body!*

Mrs. Alazar set her briefcase down while she applauded the unveiling. I walked past the open case and slipped Kelly's wish list for a normal life inside. As soon as it slipped from my fingers I was blown forward into a blur of light that had my stomach turning and slammed smack into Kelly.

"Ouch," I cried. We were back in the quad like no time had passed at all. A knot was already growing above my left eye where it had hit her binder. Kelly's stuff had spilled onto the concrete for the second time. But thanks to the backspace key, she didn't know that.

"Hey, pick those up," she cried.

"No," I braced myself for impact, trying not to shut my eyes. "Everyone has crap happen to them all the time, but you don't have to take it out on me."

"What's up your butt? I just didn't want my favorite lip gloss to roll away." Kelly bent to pick up the moving items. She dropped the gloss into her purse and then pulled out my crystal. "I think this is yours. I found it yesterday. My mom found something too. Any idea how a certain sheet of paper got into her briefcase?"

I shook my head and reached for the broken chain holding the crystal. Kelly looked straight into my eyes, then released the crystal.

I may have mumbled 'see ya' as she turned to leave. I'm not really sure. This alternate reality would take some getting used to.

Chapter 36

Even my eyelids were sore when I tried to open my eyes the next morning. When I finally focused on the clock it was already afternoon. Desperation and time travel were exhausting.

A feeling of something different plagued me for a moment. Sun. It was shining through the window. I wanted to cover my face with the blanket and stay in bed. But I had to get up.

Although the sun was shining, it was only through a small opening between dark clouds. I didn't appreciate the brilliant rainbow slicing across the sky. I had my own rainbow to get back to. No telling when the winter sun would shine again.

I grabbed a notebook and put the crystal campfire on the sill. A string of yarn worked to hold the crystal around my neck. The familiar spin began as I reclined on my pillows and was pulled toward the spiraling rainbow. I landed near the casket.

Forcing myself away from Eddie's chalky face, I scanned the large but nearly empty room.

Eddie's mother and father sat in the front pew. They held each other crying. On the right sat a different me, my face hidden behind my hands. In the back row, leaning against the wall next to a door, stood Randy. His trademark sunglasses hid his eyes, but the grim set on his face betrayed his feelings.

The door opened and I moved outside, my reflection sliding across Randy's lenses as I passed. The sun was bright and I held my hand up to shield my eyes. Two skateboarders rode by. Randy first, who yelled to Eddie to hurry up. Eddie followed and stopped in front of me, looking around as if someone had called him.

A small car with dark windows sat behind the car wash. The license plate burned into my memory. Randy pulled cash from his pocket and handed it to the driver—a thin-faced teenager with equal amount of freckles and pimples dotting his face.

The driver passed a small plastic bag to Randy then rolled away. The guys rode to the small shed behind Eddie's house. Eddie swallowed one small white pill out, then offered the bag to Randy as Mrs. Kekune called from the back porch.

Randy stuffed the bag into his pocket and swung around, knocking over several paint cans. The few words Mrs. Kekune said before she waved goodbye and closed the front door were too quiet for me to hear. Eddie and Randy ran to the front yard. They were laughing and shoving each other in the shoulder. Eddie stumbled. His knees buckled and he dropped face-first onto the sidewalk. He pushed up with one arm and rolled over on his back.

His cheek was bloody where it had scraped the concrete. One hand scratched at his shirt over his heart. Then he was still.

My hands could not touch Eddie. My voice could not call out for help. But I stayed with him when Randy ran away. I stayed until the light left his eyes and the ambulance loaded his body.

The vision cleared and the crystal necklace was so hot against my skin, I ripped it off. Nine years ago I stood helpless and watched someone die in the street. That was out of my control. This wasn't. It couldn't be. I had to save Eddie.

My hand shook so bad as I tried to write down the details, I couldn't read my own writing. I stopped and took a deep breath then recorded everything from the vision from the bright day down to the black t-shirt Eddie wore with the tear on the left sleeve.

Rubbing cramped fingers, I thought of Mom. She had seen death in the crystal too. She found a way to save me, but cost her life. What's it going to take for me to save Eddie? I put my head on my arms and cried. For Eddie. For me. For Mom.

Chapter 37

Five days of constant drizzle kept my shoes squeaking and my backpack damp and my mind spinning. Somewhere between driving me nuts and crushing on me—that baggy-pants wearing, artsy, caretaker of mothers, druggie-wanna-be became my friend. I'm driven to save Eddie. Not because of my legacy. But because I care. Crap.

Under the front eave between the wheelchair ramp and the main doors I waited for Cathy after school. Goosebumps crawled up my arms as I spotted Eddie. He rolled up the ramp on his skateboard wearing the same black t-shirt from my vision—but without the tear in the sleeve. I relaxed. Today wasn't the day.

"Hey," Eddie nodded. This was the most he'd said to me lately.

"Hey," I croaked. He grabbed his board and turned to the door. *Now or never.* "So what's up? We haven't talked in a while." *Stupid. We never really talked.* "I mean I haven't seen you around much."

"I've been hanging with Randy."

"That doesn't sound like a good idea," I said. Eddie glared. "I mean I'm sure he's a great guy and everything once you get to know him. *Gag.* But he's got a bad reputation. People might think you do what he does by being around him." From the frown on his face, cutting down his friend wasn't a good ice breaker.

"Why do you care anyway?" Eddie said. "It's not like anything I do is going to make a difference."

Although a ray of sunlight cracked between the clouds, his mood darkened. I didn't need mind reading to know he was thinking of Mr. Rush.

Randy started up the wheelchair ramp, unsteady like he was already high. I had to tell Eddie. Now.

"I c—oof!" Randy hit me as he fell off his board, grabbing Eddie's shirt on the way down.

"Hey! You ripped my favorite shirt." Eddie pulled Randy up off the ground.

"Uh!" My nerves tore with his sleeve.

"It looks better that way." Randy said. "Everything's set up for after school. Want to bring your little girlfriend along?"

"She's not my girlfriend," Eddie said.

"Then maybe she'll be mine." Randy stared in a way I wanted to cross my arms in front of my chest. *I now understand the word leer.*

"No," Eddie said as he pushed Randy's board back into his arms. "We're not her type. Let's go."

I need to do something but what? They rolled down the ramp and around the building. I willed my frozen legs to move and ran off after him. Dodging student after student in the crowded quad after school, I sprinted to Eddie, who was on the edge of the parking lot. I put my hand up to stop him while I caught my breath.

"What?" Eddie asked.

"I need to talk to you. Alone." I swallowed hard and waited for Randy to get the hint and leave. One of the longest ten seconds of my life. Randy actually winked at me before he left. My skin crawled and it had nothing to do with goose bumps. "I had a dream, and you were in it—you were with Randy. You took some kind of drug and...I know this is going to sound stupid but, well, you died."

"Died? What are you talking about? What do you mean a dream?"

"More like a vision, I guess," I squirmed, holding my voice down so the others getting into cars couldn't hear.

"You have *visions*?" Eddie laughed. "And you're worried about *me* using drugs."

"I don't use drugs!"

"I don't either," Eddie said. "Not really. Just a little pot now and then. But I know it's okay stuff."

"That's still using." I shook my head. "But it wasn't pot. It was a pill. Something was wrong with it; you grabbed your heart and died."

"You're crazy," Eddie said as he slung his backpack over his shoulder. "I don't use."

Clutching his torn sleeve I pulled. "I'm telling you—"

"Hey!" he shouted, tugging away. "I don't use!"

"Well, don't start," I screamed back.

"What do you care anyway?"

"I care, all right?" My voice softened. "You're my friend. I don't want to see this happen to you."

"Friend?" He threw his backpack at my feet. "Fine. Then why don't you tell me what's up with you, *friend*? I've seen that look on your face. I've seen things happen. What are you? Telekinetic?"

"No!" My first instinct was to protect.

"Yeah, right. And I'm not using, either." Eddie grabbed his backpack and started to roll away. *It's not like anyone cares anyway.*

There was no use trying to hide anything anymore. *He wants telekinesis, he gets telekinesis.* I concentrated on the skateboard trunk that held the back two wheels. They fell off and Eddie stumbled, but managed to stay upright.

Picking up the wheels, he walked back to me. "Did you do this?"

"It used to just happen when I was upset," I said. "Now I can sometimes make things move or break. And…I have visions."

I had his attention now. He stood perfectly still. And stared.

"Yes, visions. About people I care about. About you."

He blinked a few times but didn't say anything.

It was now or never. "The dealer drives a little silver car with black windows. His license plate reads MY XTC. He deals from behind the car wash. He's a skinny white guy with brown hair. His front tooth is trimmed with gold."

"How can you know this?" Eddie shook me by the arms. His anger scared me. "You know what would happen to you if they found out you knew?"

"I saw it, Eddie," I cried. His nails dug in through my shirt. "I pictured it clearly like I was watching TV. I can't explain how this happened to me, but I can tell you I'm afraid it's true. I saw a vision of the future and you...you were dead."

He pushed me away. "You don't know what you're talking about. These are my friends. I trust them. They're like me. They understand what it's like to be me."

"I understand what it's like to be you, too."

"Gimme a break."

"I do. I know you're mad at your dad for running out on you and your mom. I'm mad at my dad. He hasn't thought of me in seven years. But screwing up your own life isn't going to make things even with your dad."

He studied me a moment then shook his head roughly. "No! Stop messing with my mind. I don't know what you are, but I know who I am. When are you going to figure it out?"

"But Eddie?"

Randy whistled from across the lot.

"Let it go!"

"Eddie, you're my friend. Or you could be. For the first time since my mom died, I have friends."

"I have to go!" He sprinted away toward Randy.

"But Eddie—" I watched him go, completely out of arguments. *All of this power and I'm powerless.*

Chapter 38

Tears rolled down my cheeks as I watched Eddie walk away. I dropped to sit on the curb and punched Gramma's number into my cell phone. No answer.

Maybe the vision was wrong. Maybe Eddie wouldn't take the drug. *Maybe I'm making up excuses to make myself feel better.*

It wasn't like I could run after him. No way could I face down Randy or the dealer on my own. Who could go with me? Cathy? And do what? Help me beat up two guys? I'd done everything I could. I'd even trusted him with my secret. But it hadn't done any good.

I wiped my wet face dry and stood up. "There's no one," I said, even as my feet spun me and bolted for home. They knew I was lying. There was Dad.

The door slammed behind me as I raced up the stairs, stopping dead before the studio. My hand was raised, but I had to force it to turn the knob. I was about to give Dad a great reason to move me away from my home. Fresh tears rolled down my cheeks and I opened the door.

"What is it?" Dad looked up from the small easel. "Are you all right?"

"It's Eddie," I sobbed. "I know you don't like him, but he needs our help. I think he's about to buy some drugs and he may be going to use them today and I'm afraid for him but even though I tried to stop him, he's convinced Randy's his true friend. He won't listen!"

"Slow down." He rushed over and held me by the shoulders. "First, are you telling me you're using drugs?"

"No!"

"Then it sounds like it's a problem for Eddie's parents." He picked up a brush from the table and started cleaning it.

"But there's only his mom and she doesn't know. We have to help."

"I don't even know him. It's none of our business." Dad busied himself rearranging the already arranged paint brushes, his back stiff.

Frustrated, I looked around the room, my mind racing. I grabbed the unwrapped Christmas gift still sitting on the shelf and held it over my head like a game of keep away. "So if a stranger could have saved Mom you wouldn't have wanted him to?"

Dad's eyes were on the gift as he leaned back against the chair, slowly exhaling. "So, where is he?"

"Behind the car wash, I think. They were going to buy from a guy in a silver car. I think they're going to go back to his house to use them. He has a shed fixed up in the backyard."

"How do you know this?"

"I just know, okay? We have to stop him."

He grabbed his jacket. "I knew that boy was trouble. Let's go."

"Where?"

"We need to talk to Eddie's mother. If they show up, we'll deal with them."

I put the gift on his desk and then a burn of heat from the crystal at my neck made me snatch it back and carry it outside. We drove first to the vacant car wash then to Eddie's house. I jumped from the car and ran up the walk. Dad followed. Mrs. Kekune came to the door. Mr. Kekune stood behind her.

"Hello. What can I do for you?"

"Mrs. Kekune, I need to talk to you about Eddie." I shivered and tried to hold back my sobs.

"Has something happened to him?" Mrs. Kekune reached back for Mr. Kekune's hand.

"Not yet," I said, "but I'm afraid for him and there are some things you need to know about Randy. He uses drugs and I think he's trying to get Eddie into it too."

"Nonsense! I know my Eddie and he would never do that!" Mrs. Kekune drew herself up to her full height. "How dare you come here with that kind of talk."

"I hope you're right," Dad said. "But my daughter is worried. She says there's a dealer who has been working with Randy. She thinks they're meeting him today. Where is Eddie right now?"

"Out with Randy," Mrs. Kekune said. "Look, my son would never use drugs."

"I'm sorry we bothered you," Dad said. "Come on, Julie."

"I hope I'm wrong," I said. "But please, if you see the guys in the shed today, would you go out and see what they're doing?"

"I trust my son and don't need to spy on him and his friends. Goodbye."

Dad and I stood for a moment on the front porch and stared at the closed door. *Why do adults always say we need to tell them everything and then they don't believe us when we do?* We walked slowly to the car. I gave up my secret for nothing.

As I pulled the door open I froze at the sound of cans falling. Then someone screamed.

"Help, help!" It was Mrs. Kekune. We ran around the house. She was standing over a body on the long wet grass and my stomach flipped over like I'd just ridden over a huge speed bump.

I reached for a backspace key on my bracelet and pulled so hard I left a mark on my wrist. It wouldn't come off. *No!* Only one backspace a year. If I hadn't been such a jerk with Kelly, I'd be able to undo this!

Eddie stood to the side, his hands clenched into fists and his shoulders shaking.

"I told him not to," Eddie pleaded, pacing wildly. "He wouldn't listen. Now it's like Mr. Rush..."

My knees buckled and I dropped to Randy's side, picked a wet leaf off his neck and then pressed my fingers into the warm, damp skin. The only beat I could feel was my own heart, threatening to rip through my chest. I rolled him over, plugged his nose and pretended he was the Red Cross dummy in PE as my mouth was about to close in on a guy's for the first time in my life.

"Not that way!" Dad pushed me aside and used his hands to beat Randy's heart.

"I'll get the ambulance," Mr. Kekune called as he ran to the house.

Dad pumped with the heel of his hands. I leaned closer, expecting to hear him counting, but he was humming—some old disco song I think. Minutes stretched like hours as his face turned red and sweat dripped onto Randy's face. Eddie squatted next to him.

"I'll take over," Eddie offered.

"You know what you're doing?—Three, Four, Five," Dad asked without missing a beat.

"This isn't my first try." Eddie took over the compressions. "I just hope this time it works."

I didn't hear the ambulance arrive, even though the siren must have been wailing. Two paramedics pushed Eddie aside and took over. He moved next to me.

I couldn't find the words, but needed to know. *Are you all right?* No answer.

An officer pointed to Eddie. "Has he taken any?"

"No. I don't use drugs." Eddie looked directly into my eyes like he could really see who I was and desperately wanted me to see him. "My friends wouldn't let me."

"You'll need to come to the station with your parents and complete a report."

When the ambulance pulled away and I sat alone, I covered my face with my arms and started to shake. Tension rolled out of me in large tears down my cheeks. *Does someone always have to die to save someone else?*

Chapter 39

"How did you know about the dealer? Are you using drugs?" Dad started to yell as soon as I closed the car door.

"No!" My shaking hands fumbled with the buckle before it finally clicked.

"Then how did you know so much? How?" He'd never looked so angry before.

"I don't know," I stammered. *How can I explain?* "You hear things around school. It's pretty easy to tell who's using and who's dealing."

"It's that common?" He slapped his palm against the dash, leaving a hand print in the dust.

"Yeah, but that doesn't mean I do drugs. I just know what's going on."

"I had no idea. I thought this was such a small town we wouldn't have that problem. Good thing I heard about Wyoming today. I got the job. We'll leave next week."

"No!"

"Now I won't have to worry about you being exposed to this anymore," he continued, ignoring me. "We're going home to pack up right now."

"Moving won't change anything," I cried, my voice so desperately high it scratched my throat. "Drugs are everywhere, but it doesn't matter because I'm not going to use them. Don't you get it? We saved someone today. You did a good thing! We don't have to leave!"

Dad didn't answer, but I could see his fists tighten on the steering wheel—his knuckles white.

When he pulled the car into our driveway minutes later, neither of us moved. The Christmas gift sat unopened between us. I knew that arguing wasn't going to convince Dad to stay. I rubbed at the ribbon on the box as I looked out the window at the rolling hills. Tiny dots of green showed in the rows of vines. Spring was coming. A new start. I was ready for mine. There was something here, in Sonoma. I could feel its force. Maybe he might be able to feel it too.

"Take me one more place right now," I said, "and I promise if you still want to go to Wyoming afterward, I won't say another word."

"You're not out to save anymore drug users today, are you?"

"No." *I'm trying to save you.* "Take me to Jack London Park. It's at the top of the Valley."

He shrugged and backed out to the road. We drove north through heavy traffic to the small village of Glen Ellen. It was silent in the car during the five-mile drive, but my mind was racing.

I didn't know what I was looking for, or if there was anything at all. But still, I hoped.

A sign for the park pointed left up Sonoma Mountain. I watched out the window and tried to think of my mother making this same trip, so many years ago. Clusters of houses on tree-covered lots were broken by large open fields, planted in grapevines.

Dad pulled up to the main gate and rolled down his window. He paid the use fee to a ranger in a small wood hut, then parked in the large, mostly empty lot. He turned off the car and looked at me.

"Now what?" he asked.

I don't know. I picked up the gift, opened the door, and stood. To the right were the stables, to the left the walls of an old stone winery. I walked ahead to a wooden post with three signs. Three choices, three directions: Lake Walk, Wildflower Walk, and Moonstone Trail. I didn't need the new crop of goosebumps or the warmth of the crystal at my neck to tell me which way to go. All year long, the moon had pulled me forward. "Come on!"

Dad's shoulders were tense and robotic as he stiffly pulled himself from the car and walked over to me. But he wasn't looking at me. He stood frozen in front of a sign that warned of rattlesnakes in the area. "Can you tell me what we're here for?"

"This way." I moved up the trail and hoped I was right. We wound into a heavy forest, thick with short bushy trees and tall eucalyptus that dripped bark at our feet. The muddy path narrowed and began to climb through a grove of redwoods that stretched tall and straight.

Several minutes into the walk we came to a fork. There was no sign. *Great! Now which way?* A sudden laughter—a girl's—sent a shockwave of goosebumps through me. No one else was around, except Dad, who had stopped further down to read a warning about mountain lions.

"Did you hear that?" I asked.

"What?" He walked up beside me, panting. "I'm done. You need to tell me what this is all about. I'm a little out of shape for a hike. Especially after what we've been through today."

Laughter rang out from higher up the trail on my right. "Please, we have to keep going."

"No, we don't. I quit. We're going back to the house. We have a lot of packing to do."

I shook from goosebumps and frustration, but held my spot and I forced the words past the lump in my throat. "Why haven't you opened Mom's gift?"

"I don't want to hear about that again."

"But you have to. You didn't pick me and Mom up from the park all those years ago. You feel guilty, but it wasn't your fault she died. You can't blame yourself."

"Stop it, Julie."

"No!" I shook the gift in front of him. "You can't face anything in the past. Not even a gift. You've been running since Mom died. That's what has to stop."

"You don't know what you're talking about," he bit out the words. "I've been trying to keep a roof over your head."

"What roof? The one in Seattle? Flagstaff? Sonoma? Mom would've hated this. I need more than a roof. I need friends that I don't have to keep saying goodbye to. And a dad who will talk to me about my mother. I need to remember her. More than just the constant nightmares I've relived since the day she died."

"You dream about...that?" His voice was dark.

"If you can't give me those things, then I think I should go live with Gramma, or with Cathy. Dolores already said I could," or I thought she would if I asked. "At least I wouldn't have to move anymore."

"You'd leave me?"

No going back now. "You aren't giving me much of a choice, are you?"

Dad's face darkened and his mind was unreadable.

"Look," I said, "when Mom came to Sonoma with Gramma, they visited this park. Mom went on a hike alone. I think this was the way she went. I need to follow her steps."

Dad shook his head sadly. "There's no use dredging up the past."

What? That's all he ever does. Goosebumps tingled over my skin and raced down my arms to my hand where I still held the gift. He needed a big push back into life. "You know, I understand you're afraid of rattlesnakes and mountain lions. Who isn't? But fear of Christmas gifts?"

Dad's chin raised up a notch. "It's not that I'm afraid."

"Then prove it." I held the package out.

His hands shook as he took it from me and pulled the ribbon free. He held a corner of the paper and paused.

"Open it!"

He slid the wrapping off and gasped. Or else the sound came from me. He held a photo of Mom. She looked about nine-months pregnant. But it wasn't the basketball sized bump that caught my attention. It was her glowing face. I had never seen another picture that truly caught my mother's happiness.

"That's it," Dad gasped, his hand to his chest. Then he stroked the photo through the glass with his fingertips. "I've been trying to capture that look for so long. I couldn't do it. And it was here, all along."

"It's like she knew what you most needed," I blubbered through my tears. "I feel really close to Mom in Sonoma. I know it sounds weird, but for some reason, I think something on this trail may tell me why."

Dad brushed a tear off my cheek. His touch was warm and fatherly, but I froze. I couldn't remember the last time he'd touched me.

"Lead on," Dad's voice cracked.

Chapter 40

The hill steepened and my legs began to burn, but I continued to climb for another twenty minutes, pulled by the belief that I'd find an answer and pushed by the fear that I would not. The path narrowed and the wet branches scratched at my arms as I neared the top. At a small bridge that crossed a rushing creek full from the weeks of rain I stopped to let Dad catch up. The water splashed over rocks as it made its way down the hill. I remembered everything clearly from my vision. I knew where I was heading, just not where I was going.

His labored breath was loud as he lumbered up the trail. I had no idea what he was thinking and I was already too emotional to look into his thoughts. He didn't take his eyes off the picture, which slowed his progress. Excitement and anxiety filled me. I was close to something—I just didn't know what.

When he reached the bridge I heard the same joyous giggle and continued upward without waiting for him to catch his breath. Minutes later, the brush-lined path turned sharply right and opened to a small clearing. In the center sat a large rock, covered with writing—names, hundreds of them.

"Hey, you two," a voice called.

I jumped at the sound. A tall gray-haired ranger entered the clearing. "The park gate is closing soon. You'd better hustle back down the hill."

Dad was bent over with had one hand on his knee as tried to catch his breath.

 The ranger stepped forward and stood beside me. "Quite a rock, isn't it? People have been adding their marks to it since way before London bought the land. Legend goes that those whose names appear on the Moonstone will find lasting love and happiness together here in the Valley." He turned back to the path. "You'd better get a move on. You don't want your car locked up all night."

Goosebumps danced over my shoulders. I knew Mom had been here, but how was that going to help me? How would it keep Dad in Sonoma?

"I bet she wrote her name, too," I said. "Help me find it."

The rock reached more than a foot above Dad's head. "It's like finding a needle in a haystack," he said. But he was already circling to the right, studying the names.

The growing goosebumps and my rapidly beating heart lead me to the left. My teeth began to chatter and a sudden lump expanded in my throat. "H-here," I choked and touched the letters with my fingers.

Dad came up behind me and gasped. His hand shook as it reached up to touch the letters. There in the rock read, "Welcome Home Drew and Jewel Anne, Love, Marina."

"That's impossible," Dad said. "When your mother came to Sonoma, we had just met. This must be someone else."

"Two other people with the names Drew and Jewel Anne?" I sobbed. "How do you explain it?"

"I can't."

Tears streamed down my face, but I was smiling. I understood. My mother had given me the power of the moon and a place to call home.

"Mom was just my age when she came here. She already knew you'd be together." I wiped the tears away. "She knew the two of you would have a daughter and name her Jewel Anne. She was right. She wanted us to end up here. I think she's right about that, too."

"Unbelievable," Dad whispered.

"Can we please stay?" My voice trembled. "Dad?"

He nodded as he dried his wet cheeks with the back of one hand and then opened his arms. I stepped closer and for the first time in years, felt like I was being hugged by both my father and my mother at the same time.

Dad's voice cracked when he spoke, "Let's go home."

Watch for

Crystal Bound 2: Power

Coming in 2011!